Ronald Knox and The Mu⌐⌐⌐ ⌐oom

››› This title is part of The Murder Room, our series dedicated to making available out-of-print or hard-to-find titles by classic crime writers.

Crime fiction has always held up a mirror to society. The Victorians were fascinated by sensational murder and the emerging science of detection; now we are obsessed with the forensic detail of violent death. And no other genre has so captivated and enthralled readers.

Vast troves of classic crime writing have for a long time been unavailable to all but the most dedicated frequenters of second-hand bookshops. The advent of digital publishing means that we are now able to bring you the backlists of a huge range of titles by classic and contemporary crime writers, some of which have been out of print for decades.

From the genteel amateur private eyes of the Golden Age and the femmes fatales of pulp fiction, to the morally ambiguous hard-boiled detectives of mid twentieth-century America and their descendants who walk our twenty-first century streets, The Murder Room has it all. **›››**

The Murder Room
Where Criminal Minds Meet

themurderroom.com

Ronald Arbuthnott Knox (1888–1957)

It was Ronald Knox, who, as a pioneer of Golden Age detective fiction, codified the rules of the genre in his 'Ten Commandments of Detection', which stipulated, among other rules, that 'No Chinaman must figure in the story', and 'Not more than one secret room or passage is allowable'. He was a Sherlock Holmes aficionado, writing a satirical essay that was read by Arthur Conan Doyle himself, and is credited with creating the notion of 'Sherlockian studies', which treats Sherlock Holmes as a real-life character. Educated at Eton and Oxford, Knox was ordained as priest in the Church of England but later entered the Roman Catholic Church. He completed the first Roman Catholic translation of the Bible into English for more than 350 years, and wrote detective stories in order to supplement the modest stipend of his Oxford Chaplaincy.

The Viaduct Murder
The Three Taps
The Footsteps at the Lock
The Body in the Silo
Still Dead
Double Cross Purposes

The Body in the Silo

Ronald Knox

An Orion book

Copyright © Lady Magdalen Asquith 1933

The right of Ronald Knox to be identified as the author of this work
has been asserted in accordance with the Copyright, Designs and
Patents Act 1988.

This edition published by
The Orion Publishing Group Ltd
Orion House
5 Upper St Martin's Lane
London WC2H 9EA

An Hachette UK company
A CIP catalogue record for this book is available from the British Library

ISBN 978 1 4719 0045 7

www.orionbooks.co.uk

To Ironica

Note to Readers

In keeping with the spirit of 'fair play' apparent in his Decalogue, or Ten Commandments of Detective Fiction, the author includes a series of footnotes towards the end of this book – as the solution to the mystery unfolds – that point the reader back to a breadcrumb trail of clues.

CONTENTS

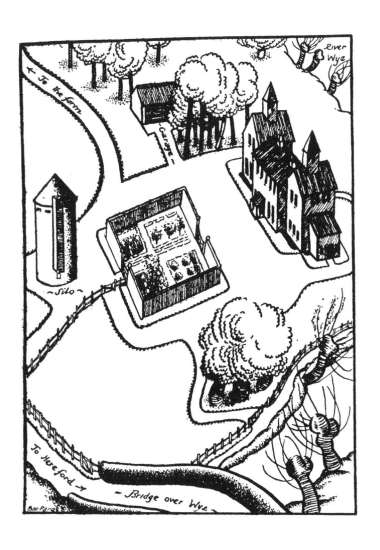

Tuesday Night.

9.30. Worsley leaves drawing-room.

10.10. Worsley rings.

10.20. Halliford goes to open gate.

10.30. Mrs. Halliford drives to the gate, returning about 10.35.

11.0. Race starts.

11.10. Tollard drops out.

11.40. Phyllis Morel stopped by police.

12.15. Tollard returns (by his own account).

12.25. Phyllis Morel passes a car, which she believes to be Tollard's.

12.30. Phyllis Morel returns to Lastbury.

12.45. Tollard returns (by Phyllis Morel's account).

12.58. The Bredons reach King's Norton.

3.0. General return to Lastbury.

" IT's NO USE," said Miles Bredon. " The
man's a bore, and the woman's a pest, and if I
did ever say I'd go there I must have been
drunk at the time. Let us leave it at that."
It is one of the drawbacks of the happiest
marriage – and his was a happy marriage – that
husband and wife are expected to go and stay
with other husbands and wives. Men on the
whole prefer their own firesides, where the
same drinks are to be had, the same books
within reach, the same disposition of pipe-
cleaners, match-boxes and envelopes is to be
expected. Women on the whole prefer one
another's ; it saves the weekly books, and all
the multitudinous worries of housekeeping,
while the expedition lasts – I assume, of course,
as you could assume with the Bredons, that an
ideal nurse reigns in the nursery. The argument now in progress was a common one ; it
ranged over a question of fact, whether the
invitation had been accepted with or without
Miles's consent ; a question of values, whether
it was worth spending three or four days of

1

what looked like promising summer weather in the house of casual acquaintances ; a question of policy, whether some excuse should not be dug up for cancelling the acceptance after all.

" You were, rather, as far as I can remember," admitted Angela. " I can't always wait till you come round. The pity was that I didn't give you an extra glass to lay you out, put you straight in the car, and decant you at the Hallifords' there and then. A sensible wife would always cart her husband about the country in a sack."

" Now I come to think of it, I don't believe I can have been as drunk as all that. To want to go and stay with the Hallifords, a man who's all Adam's apple and front teeth, and a woman who's all colours of the rainbow, at a place on the Welsh border where there probably isn't a golf-course within miles – no, you must have misunderstood me."

" It's no use crabbing the Hallifords ; that's not the point. They're your friends, not mine."

" My friends ? Listen to her ! You know perfectly well that they scraped an acquaintance with me through Sholto ; and how the mischief they knew I was connected with the Indescribable beats me. People aren't supposed to know that kind of thing, and I believe I could get Sholto the sack if I told the Directors he had been giving away their little games.

Oh, Mr. Bredon, I've always wanted to meet a real detective – blast her ! "

Once again, for the benefit of the illiterate, I must take up my pen to describe the Indescribable, and to define Bredon's indefinable relation to it. The Indescribable is *the* insurance company, compared with which the other insurance companies all look like last year's models. It was the Indescribable which paid up, merely for the advertisement, when a large hotel in South America took out a policy against earthquakes and was blown down, while in building, by a tornado ; it was the Indescribable which underwrote the recent attempt to cross from Durazzo to Brindisi in a canoe ; there was a rumour, but the thing was never acknowledged, that they were prepared to insure a belligerent minor state against all indemnities it would incur by going to war, only the League of Nations stepped in at the last moment. Such is the Indescribable Company ; it likes taking big risks and taking risks on a large scale. It also likes charging big premiums.

Miles Bredon was its private detective. To be sure, such an adjunct was not absolutely necessary. Those who set out to defraud insurance companies render themselves thereby liable to prosecutions which are instituted, at the taxpayer's expense, by the police. But the police do not always find it advisable to prosecute, and a company does not always find it advisable to contest a fishy claim. It paid the Indescribable, therefore, to keep their own private inquiry agent, who would go round and ferret out the facts, so that they could be sure where they stood. The position was well paid, and the man who held it was an ex-officer who was a good deal cleverer than he admitted. But for some reason he held that his profession was the degrading profession of a spy, and did his best not to let it be talked about. In this the company nobly seconded his efforts; their "representative," Mr. Bredon, appeared on suitable occasions, but they were not anxious that his precise position in the economy of the business should be made public.

This time, it seemed, a leak had occurred. A Mr. Halliford, calling at the offices of the Indescribable to effect a very heavy insurance on his own life, had demanded to see "that clever fellow Bredon, who made such a good job of the Burtell business." I cannot stop to explain about the Burtell business, but Halliford, anyhow, was a friend of Mr. Nigel Burtell, who (for reasons elsewhere given) had a higher opinion of Mr. and Mrs. Bredon than they had of him. It happened that Bredon was in the office; the authorities of the Company, always anxious to make a good customer feel at home, insisted that he should come up and be introduced, not only to Halliford himself, but to the lady whom he had just married. In this Mr. Halliford did not stand alone ; a certain exotic charm and a volatile temperament had already endowed the lady with a rich supply of matrimonial aliases. Bredon loathed her at sight ; loathed her still more when, through sheer importunacy, she secured his presence and that of his wife Angela at a dinner in her London flat. And now the third wave was threatening ; nor can we judge Bredon hardly if he showed symptoms of wanting to retire up the beach.

Angela, however, was inexorable. " I don't think it's quite nice to talk like that of a woman who will be so rich when her husband dies," she pointed out. " How much did you say it was ? Eighty thousand ? "

" That was the figure. But, you see, the Indescribable doesn't insure people against divorce ; and I fancy Mrs. H. will have run through several other husbands before we have to cough up the claim. Are you really going to take me to stay with that woman ? You can't even pretend there's anything to be said for her."

" Of course, she's pretty." Angela spoke in that ruminating voice which wives use when they want their husbands to contradict them on such points as these.

" The great detective," Bredon pointed out,

" is expected to be able to see through all dis-
guises. But then, I'm not a great detective,
and Mrs. Halliford . . ."

" Charitable as always. Well, anyhow,
you're for it. I've never been to Herefs, and
I hear great things of it. Probably there will
be golf somewhere, there always is ; and there
will be lots of other ways to keep in training.
She says something in her letter about a scavenging party ; that ought to be a good opening
for a man who wants to keep his hand in at
detection."

" A scavenging party – what on earth's that ? "

" Miles, dear, don't be old-fashioned. A
scavenging party is when you go round in cars
picking up tramps by the roadside and feeding
them fish and chips at Much Wenlock ; or
collecting sandwich-boards and doorscrapers
and things like that. All the brightest young
people do it."

" Sort of thing the Hallifords would do, anyhow. Those are the people who make one so
sick of England ; people who make money in
oil or something, and buy up the old houses
where decent people lived before them, who had
a stake in the country and knew their tenants
and preserved and drank port and lived natural
lives. These people play tennis instead of
cricket . . ."

" Why not ? "

6

" Don't interrupt me ; I'm in the middle of a speech. It isn't that I mind tennis, but it hasn't got the tradition value of cricket. Who ever heard of somebody refusing to do a shady thing on the ground that it wasn't tennis? And of course these modern people wouldn't refuse, anyhow. They play tennis with their rich friends instead of cricket on the village green with the blacksmith at one end and the second footman at the other. And instead of hunting hounds, or even subscribing, they tear round the countryside in cars making themselves a nuisance to everybody. Of course we breed Bolsheviks ; who wouldn't be a Bolshevik when he's expected to go and stay with a long-necked man who spends his time pinching other people's doorscrapers? "

" Oh, Miles, I wish you'd been one of those old-fashioned rich people who played cricket. Think what a lovely magistrate you'd have been, if you can make speeches like that. Mr. Bredon, in remanding the prisoner, called attention to the growing habit of doorscraper-pinching, to which he attributed the falling off of enlistments in the local territorials. And you would write letters to the papers, and I would correct the spelling for you. However, it's no good worrying over what might have been. What's got to be is that Annie's mother is ill and I've got to let her go off home, and

7

while she's away I've got to have you looked after by somebody else's housemaids. You may not think the Hallifords much class, but their invitation was a godsend just now. And it's Herefs for us to-morrow."

" Trust you to get out of it on a technicality of some kind. Why didn't you tell me about the domestic crisis before ? And answer me this if you can ; why on earth do the Hallifords want us there ? Why did they rout me out at the office and send us about six invitations to dine ? We aren't their sort ; we don't know the people they know ; and it's going to cost more in petrol getting there than it would cost getting in a deputy housemaid. Well, well, have it your own way. But remember, I take the patience cards. It isn't a business expedition this time."

What good things Angela had been told about Herefordshire did not transpire, but certainly on a flawless day of summer it endeared itself by its approach. Sudden, conical hills thickly wooded, old grey archways that had once been lodge gates, pointing along grass-grown roads up avenues now meaningless, farmhouses older and more substantial than is our English wont, vistas, as you climbed a hill, of hops stretching across the fields, row upon row, like Venetian blinds ; orchards of whitened trunks and fruit-laden boughs, little brick-and-timber villages huddling round duckponds, tall hedges with white-faced cows at the gaps in them looking at you with an outraged expression, as if they suspected you of being after the doorscraper – it was holiday enough, this afternoon drive, whatever hospitality awaited them at the end of it. There is a remoteness, a tuckedawayness, about our countryside where (especially) England of the English marches with her neighbours ; here towns were scarce, and abbeys and bridges, because living was unsettled, and except where some accident of modern industrialism has intervened there are no landmarks to distinguish to-day from yesterday ; only the rare castles lie in ruins, and there are no Roman roads, no remembered battlefields.

Above all, when they reached it, the Wye had this atmosphere of seclusion. The road is for ever travelling close to it, as roads must when there is hilly country to be traversed, but always at just so much interval as gave you only tantalising glimpses of it ; *secretum meum mihi*, it said, and kept you at a distance. The modernity of the bridges reminded you that it was not meant for traffic to cross ; a ford here, a ferry there, had been enough till the other day to serve its rustic neighbours. The banks sloping precipitately, with trees older and more spreading than such as love the companionship of rivers, a bare scarp, sometimes, of red cliff rising two hundred feet out of the stream, hurrying rapids alternating with deep pools where the salmon jumped noisily – of all this they caught only an occasional view, but enough to whet their appetite for closer exploration. Certainly it seemed hard on this patient countryside, so far from London that the very speech of its inhabitants came near to the pitch-accent of the barbarian Welsh, that the Hallifords and their friends should have descended upon it ; that their gramophones should pierce the stillness of its woods, their motor-boats foul the river, their metropolitan vulgarity drive the labourer further than ever into himself, further than ever away from the masters who hired his service. All this, be sure, Bredon rubbed into his wife relentlessly, and suggested more than once that they should lose their way, put up at a village inn somewhere, and have the country all to themselves.

They did lose their way in the end, through the fault of an optimistic cartographer who promised them short cuts across a district with which he was plainly unfamiliar. Lastbury, the village for which they were making, disappeared suddenly from the signposts, and their informants bewildered them, as such informants will, by assuming a knowledge of the local landmarks which only a native could possess. In the end, they found that Lastbury Hall was a more natural objective than Lastbury village ; it was impossible to miss it, once you were within a mile or two, you would see the silo standing out as plain as you would wish among the trees, " Like as it might be a church tower," one imaginative mind suggested. And it was, finally, what looked like a round church tower that identified their destination for them. Telegraph wires pointed towards it, and it seemed clear that they were going to strike a farm road into the estate. " But," insisted Bredon, still unenlightened, " what on earth is a silo ? "

IF BREDON HAD kept in his car – and what
could possibly be more useful ? – a copy of
Larousse Universel, he would have been able to
pick up a lot of knowledge about silos, most of
which would have been misleading for his
present purposes. He would have learned that
a silo is a subterranean ditch where one puts
down the grains, the vegetables, etc., to con-
serve them ; that there is a punishment existing
in the army of North Africa which consists in
shutting up the condemned in a silo ; that silos
were known by the ancients, and that traces of
them still exist, remarkable for their imperme-
ability. That the name is used, by extension,
of airy reservoirs in cement, etc., in which
one immagazines the grains while waiting for
their loading on boats or waggons. Finally,
after much else, that these airy silos (for the
grains, the minerals, etc.) are hermetically
sealed and carry dispositives of mechanical
brewage to assure the conservation of the grains.
Nothing would have prepared him for finding a

12

large building made like a lighthouse, forty feet high, with no windows, except a skylight in its conical top, no door, and indeed no opening at all except on one side, where a series of square hatches, one above another, led right up to the roof.

His thirst for information was fortunately in a good way to be satisfied. At the foot of the building stood Mr. Halliford, who was even then explaining the silo, a recent and favourite toy, to one of his guests. This was a young man with pronounced horn-rimmed spectacles, whom Bredon suspected, with justice as it proved, of being an author. His manner and costume did not suggest that he was a ready audience for agricultural homilies, and it seemed only decent to leave the car and express polite interest. "Know Mr. Tollard? Mr. and Mrs. Bredon. I was just telling Mr. Tollard about the silo. Get all my stuff stored in there for the winter, stuff for the cattle, I mean. It ferments in there, you see, and keeps as sweet as possible all the year round, like preserved fruit, you know. Cattle get so fond of it, you have to drive 'em off it when the spring comes before they'll look at grass ; positively. You'll see the men filling it to-morrow."

"Stinks rather," observed Mr. Tollard, who felt that something was due from him in the way of conversation.

" Stinks ? You bet it does ; gas coming off all the time. You have to be careful in there, people have been overpowered and poisoned in silos before now. And of course you have to have men standing in there to spread it out level ; otherwise you get air-pockets and it goes bad through not fermenting evenly. Of course, if I was really up to date I should have a proper machine to pile it with ; looks in over the top, you know, for all the world like an elephant's trunk. But we hoist up the bundles by that pulley there – good strong pulley, that is ; take any amount of weight – and the platform by the skylight is hinged, so that it makes way for the sacks when they come up, and falls back into place to receive them. The men climb up by that ladder – you *can* climb up by the traps, of course, but it's a nuisance. Well, it's no good looking at it now, because the men have knocked off work ; come down to-morrow if you're interested. You must be tired, Mrs. Bredon, after that long drive ; come up to the house ; there's tea there and things."

Lastbury Hall, like several other houses in those parts, has paid in Victorian architecture the price of its Victorian prosperity. The old farmhouse – it was hardly more – was burned down in the sixties, and was replaced by a considerable, though not uncomfortably large, mansion (I use the word advisedly) in a style

which can only be characterised as imitation
Pugin. Bad red bricks, badly laid, stretched
this way and that with unrelieved surface, save
where they were broken by arched windows,
innocent of depth and moulding. Slate
pinnacles crowned the roof, reminiscent of our
nursery boxes of " stone bricks " ; the house
was too high for its area, too shallow to admit
of comfortably sized rooms ; the windows fitted
badly, after the fashion of Victorian Gothic
windows ; the chimneys were out of proportion
but could never be persuaded not to smoke.
And this regrettable incident of modern architecture faced squarely, across a precipitous
lawn, to the lovely deep pools of the Wye, along
which a path ran, the envy of river-farers,
roofed with ancient trees, fringed with meadow-
sweet and wild Canterbury bells. To enjoy
this view, which they had done so little to
deserve, the earlier owners of the house had
thrown out a hideous iron verandah, the lower
part of it mercifully hidden in rambler roses.
It was here that the Bredons were presented to
their hostess and to a group of guests who
struggled uneasily out of their deck chairs.

Mrs. Halliford was a synthetic blonde whose
schoolgirl complexion was startlingly ill matched
to the extreme frailness of her physique. Her
welcome, and her alternative offer of tea and
cocktails was embarrassed by the persistence

of a wasp which she kept on waving away in obvious alarm. " I do so hate them, don't you, Mrs. Bredon ? And the funny thing is I can never bring myself to kill them. No, don't, Phyllis, don't squash it ; I can't bear to see a squashed wasp. Wait till it's settled, and I'll get this cup over it. . . . There, now it can't get out. Too bad, on a perfect afternoon like this."

" They don't really settle if you leave 'em alone," said her husband.

" You wouldn't say that if you used lip stick," objected the lady addressed as Phyllis. " I'm all for killing them. No idea you were so fond of animals, Myrtle."

" Who, me ? No, I've no pity for the wasps ; it's just that I can't bear scrunchiness. No, I wouldn't mind if all the animals in the world were destroyed except my darling Alexis. He looks as if he thought there were too many animals in the world at the moment. Stop scratching, Alexis, and come over here to be introduced."

A large black monkey came out from the open window, with that sinister air monkeys have of knowing exactly which member of the party they mean to bite, only not wanting to give away the fun beforehand. It looked at Angela as if she were the last straw in a miserable world, then seemed to give up the idea that there was any entertainment to be had and swarmed up a pillar of the verandah.

" Isn't he a pet ? " said Mrs. Halliford.

" I can't ever think of monkeys as pets, somehow," Angela explained. " They look so human that I always feel as if I was insulting them by offering to scratch them or anything. And that absurd trick of looking unhappy gives me the hump rather. Is he clever ? "

" He can imitate anything. Of course, he never will show off in company. But it's a scream to see him pretending to read the newspaper and dusting the pictures. He watches the servants, you know, early in the morning. The other day he tore up all our letters before we got down to breakfast, didn't you, my precious? Walter was rather angry about it, but it was all right really, because there were no cheques."

" Do you leave him loose all the time ? "

" Oh yes, except when he's shut up for the night. He's perfectly harmless. Now, what about some bridge ? "

Mrs. Halliford, it proved, was one of those hostesses who are too fond of managing things ; her suggestions were made with a shade too much of confidence, so that it seemed just not polite to refuse them. Not that in this case the invitation was likely to fall on deaf ears ; except for Miles himself the company rose with as

17

much alacrity as a hot afternoon and deck chairs would allow. Angela sat talking to Mrs. Halliford ; and if the reader is inclined to complain that he would have liked more conversation, by way of getting the characters put in their places, he is invited instead to watch them as they play bridge, with that inscrutable look which so admirably betrays the characters of card-players, and hear Mrs. Halliford's own explanation of them as she poured it out to Angela. So frank were her descriptions that Angela began to feel as if she would be a dangerous friend to have, and wondered what the Bredon *dossier* sounded like when they were not among those present.

Mr. Tollard, it seemed, whom we have already met, was a young author of the kind that seems to make a reasonable living by that precarious trade without any great splash of publicity. Nobody had ever hailed him as the hope of the English novel or credited him with having taken up the mantle of Mr. Galsworthy. You did not see his works dotted over the bookstalls, nor on the other hand did you see fabulous prices quoted for his first editions. He was a safe seller, and no publisher feared to lose money over him. The notoriety he possessed, or had possessed, was of a different and less fortunate kind. Some five years before, as a very young man, he had gone out to the United States, and, in one of those cities whose hectic living is the delight of our Sunday papers, he had got into considerable unpleasantness. A man who had openly threatened to ruin him was found shot ; he had died by his own hand, the jury decided in the end, but it was after a long and thoroughly sensational trial, which left some mud sticking to Mr. Tollard, and cleared him of guilt without altogether clearing him of suspicion. He was gradually living down the fame of the event in this country of short memories. Mrs. Halliford dwelt on the harmlessness of his present character much as you would exonerate a dog which has once been caught sheep-stealing ; it was evident that she did not share the jury's opinion. Mr. Tollard wrinkled his eyebrows a good deal over each hand and was altogether more demonstrative, you would say, than the rigour of the game demands. In person he was slight, in complexion sallow, but he was not ill-looking, and a humorous mouth lent grace to his sardonic habit of speech.

Phyllis Morel, who was his partner, was a friend of Mrs. Halliford's, who talked of her with something approaching affection. Half French, and the daughter of an unhappy marriage, she had long had to fend for herself, and, being " motor-mad," took to running a garage with the little property she possessed. The thing was a success, and Phyllis, who at first had not disdained to work in overalls on the premises, was now a largely absentee director, amusing herself with hair-raising speed trials. She looked healthy and natural, by contrast at least with her hostess ; and she had a faculty, rare among women, of swearing without seeming affected when she did so. Something Mrs. Halliford said gave Angela the idea that she and Tollard were being thrown together, but it was not quite clear why or by whom.

The Carberrys were their host's friends ; their hostess did not profess to know them very well, but retailed all there was to be known about them. John Carberry had been a friend of Halliford's in South Africa (where he made his money) and had only recently come back to England, by no means a rich man himself. Rough diamonds, said Mrs. Halliford, one was accustomed to, especially among South Africans, " but I think it's such a pity to be rough without being a diamond, don't you ? " And indeed he was of an unrestrained vulgarity which an earlier society would have felt remarkable in such surroundings. He contradicted with no semblance of apology, and lectured his unfortunate partner, Mrs. Arnold, with an acerbity from which her sex should have protected her, though her play demanded it. He had been in the mining business when he had

first known her husband, but was now in the
City, with an itch for company promoting and
very little safe income. He had married " somebody out there " – a woman who had been
decidedly pretty but was now inclined to stout-
ness, good-natured and jolly, but a bit flashy,
as Mrs. Bredon would see for herself. Angela
rather liked her looks, and felt for her – she
was so evidently conscious of her husband's
social inadequacy, always watching for a *gaffe*
and always toning down the level of general
conversation so that he should be able to chime
in without remark. She won confidence, later,
by talking about her two sons at school, to
whom she was inordinately attached.

The Arnolds were a wizened pair by contrast ;
she, a woman with a permanent grievance,
who seldom opened her mouth without making
you aware of it ; he, a flaxen-haired man with
a weak mouth and harassed eyes. They were
connections, it seemed, of Mr. Halliford's ; and
Mrs. Halliford never felt at her ease with them
because from their point of view she was a
disaster – she had come between them and the
possibility of inheriting her husband's money.
How was it ? – oh, yes, Mrs. Arnold's mother
had been Halliford's cousin, so there was no
close relationship ; but to hear her talk you
would think Walter – that was Mr. Halliford –
had been a kind of trustee for a fortune that

21

was due to come to them. "And he has provided for them in his will, you know – much too generously, *I* think." The Arnolds lived not far off and descended often on Lastbury Hall ; they had been asked to stay more for the sake of a party than because there were any lost threads of intimacy to be picked up. Leslie Arnold belonged to the county, coming from a hopelessly cadet branch of an old family, and was a landowner in a very small way. "He knows about cows and things," explained Mrs. Halliford, as if feeling that there ought to be some justification for his existence. On a better acquaintance, Angela put him down as a scholar and something of a dreamer by temperament, forced to pose as a man of the world through his wife's perpetual pre-occupation with the family finances.

"And that's the whole party," Mrs. Halliford concluded, "except of course Cecil Worsley. What ! Didn't I tell you Cecil Worsley was going to be here ? Oh yes, he often comes here ; he's quite an old friend of mine. He comes by train, and we expect him any minute now. You're sure to like Cecil ; he's such good company.".

CECIL WORSLEY WAS one of those people who make England what she is in the world. They also make you wonder who in the world they are. Not more than a thousand people, probably, knew him by sight, but he was in the very middle of things. He counted among the people who counted ; he influenced their opinion more than most departments in the Civil Service can, and much, much more than the electorate.

It is difficult to describe him except by a long litany of negations. He was comfortably off but not in any way noticeably rich. He was of decent family but nowhere within reasonable distance of a peerage ; nor had his connections helped him at all in his rise to position. He had brains, to be sure, and a brilliant academic career behind him ; but anybody who watches brilliant academic careers knows that about ninety per cent. of them lead to nothing. He did not control any business interests ; he did not edit a newspaper – not, I mean, the kind of newspaper which anybody reads. He had never stood for Parliament or appeared on platforms on his friends' behalf. He was neither a Civil Servant nor a banker, such as are principally engaged just now in building up the kingdom of heaven on earth. He had the *entrée* of many great houses, but seldom availed himself of the privilege ; you did not see photographs of him in the papers watching the races at Gatwick or sun-bathing on the Riviera. *Who's Who* found space for his name, but told you nothing whatever about him except that he collected old china. Most of what he wrote was anonymous ; most of his important interviews were conducted over the luncheon table. Nobody knew whether he was a Liberal, a Conservative or a Socialist ; whether he was a believer or an atheist. It seemed out of place to raise such issues when you were talking about Cecil Worsley.

But he counted enormously. His visits, not chronicled by the newspapers, to New York or to Geneva ; his unsigned articles, his advice to politicians, his selection of the right candidate for the next vacant post – you could not exaggerate his influence. Angela, though she concealed her ignorance, had never heard of him. Her husband, to whom much of the conversation already recorded was repeated as they dressed for dinner, knew that one ought to know about him, but little more. Both alike wondered what he could be doing in a party like this, so remote from everything that was fashionable, from everything that was official. The explanation as Angela heard it next day was simple ; he was a very old friend of Mrs. Halliford's, and he often came down to Lastbury to take a rest from the great world which, to him, meant business. And indeed his whole manner was that of the favoured guest, who gets up and leaves the room almost without noticing his company, reads a book while conversation is general, goes out for walks by himself, and comes home late for meals. None the less, he could throw himself into his surroundings, and fraternised with the miscellaneous party at dinner without a trace of condescension.

" I'm so sorry we had to fetch you up in the Bridge," Mrs. Halliford said to him. " Toto is out of order as usual, and Walter won't keep another respectable car. I'm really ashamed of it when we have to use it for visitors. It's quite comfortable, though."

" And runs well," said Worsley. " I didn't know they made these things with such good engines."

" It must have bumped a bit on some of these side roads," suggested Bredon. " You've one or two bad patches round here, Mrs. Halliford."

" Well, we must be thankful for the main ones," said Worsley. " A couple of centuries ago, I believe, the roads were so bad in this county that they were perfectly impassable all the winter. If you came to stay in October or thereabouts, you had to make it a four months' visit. Must have been trying for the hosts."

" Oh, but that sounds delightful," protested Mrs. Halliford. " You must come again in the late autumn, Mr. Bredon, and we'll have the drive dug up on purpose to keep you here. I hope you found your way all right ? People generally get lost the first time they come."

" Oh, we got lost all right, but people kept on directing us to the silo. It seems to be a kind of Admiralty landmark in these parts. You've put Lastbury on the map, Mrs. Halliford."

" Ah, that's all very well, but I'd sooner have a village church nestling in the trees, with lots of ancestors buried there. I'd give my soul to be like the Vyners and have places called Sutton Vyner and Milton Vyner dotted all round me. So feudal."

" It's an odd thing, that," observed Worsley. " One of the main differences between England and Scotland – in England biography is the key to geography ; in Scotland it's the other way about."

" Say that again, Cecil, in words of one syllable. I'm not there."

" Oh, it's quite simple. I only mean that in England the big families have attached their names to places ; if you were called Smith the village you lived in was called Muddleford Smith to distinguish it from Muddleford Parva. In Scotland, if a younger son of the McNabs built himself a wretched little shooting-lodge at Strathbogle, his descendants called themselves McNabs of Strathbogle in perpetuity. How did Shakespeare know his Scotland so well? *Glamis hath murdered sleep, and therefore Cawdor shall sleep no more* – you would never find Shakespeare talking about Lord Burghley as Hatfield."

"He's always bringing in Welshmen, too, isn't he?" put in Phyllis Morel, who was sitting next to Bredon. "There was one came in the *Merry Wives of Windsor*; I looked it up the other day, when we were doing the charades, for Falstaff. Do you remember, Myrtle, what a job we had getting Walter into the clothes-basket?"

"Do you fish?" Mrs. Halliford asked Bredon. She had a habit, he thought, of changing the subject rather suddenly.

"No, I'm afraid not. I play golf, you know, and I think one ought to do one thing or the other, not both. I suppose it's salmon fishing here? We saw them jumping in the pools."

"Yes, it's good salmon fishing. Though they're not taking, Walter says. I can't bear it; I couldn't bear golf, either – too slow. I want speed, all the time."

"Funny you should say that," observed Worsley. "I was thinking about it only just

27

now, as I came up in that very speedy Bridge ; I passed a man on a horse, just riding it on business, which always looks so old-fashioned nowadays. I was wondering whether the new generation as a whole is different, or whether it's just a class of people who have come into their own. I mean, one used to assume that one's nerves wanted relaxing, so one went and did something slow, like fishing. Now, people seem to want something which braces the nerves instead – to prevent them screaming, I suppose. Is that because our nerves are getting more acute, or what?"

" *I* don't want speed to brace my nerves," objected Miss Morel. " I want it for its own sake."

" *Speed, speed, speed in the knees of the Lord ?* " suggested Worsley. " I never could quite understand how Henley managed to lug theology into it."

" Phyllis is like that," admitted Mrs. Halliford. " But with me I think it's just wanting to go faster than other people. I always go all out to catch up any car that's ahead of me ; I believe I'd do the same in a donkey-cart – with the other donkey-carts, I mean."

" I suppose that's the fun of scavenging parties," suggested Bredon, avoiding his wife's eye. He knew that she was registering disgust at his hypocrisy ; hadn't he, only yesterday, disclaimed all knowledge of the things ? But, dash it all, one must live up to one's company.

" Oh, you heard about ours ? Of course, we went in for treasure-hunts originally, but the neighbours were rather tiresome about it. Basil Freeland got one of the clues wrong, and dug up rows and rows of potatoes. They belonged to the sweetest old man in side whiskers and a square bowler hat, but he wasn't at all pleased about it. So we took to scavenging parties instead."

" Did you have any good ones ? " asked Tollard, who was sitting just beyond Phyllis Morel. " I was in one the other day where we had to collect clergymen."

" That sounds difficult," said Phyllis. " How did you manage yours ? "

" Oh, I left him till last ; then I cruised along near the Abbey till I saw a short-sighted one looking lost, and shouted, *Taxi, Sir* ? He thought it was all right at first, but he got restive in the suburbs, and he wasn't nice about it, though we only took them out to Staines."

" One seems to be able to do anything in London," complained Mrs. Halliford. " Down here, people are so touchy. We collected blackboards the other day, from the village schools, you know, which I thought was rather a good idea, though poor James Lawson, who's so deaf, wasted quite a lot of time catching a blackbird. You wouldn't have thought any-body would have minded, because we gave them back afterwards; indeed, I don't think the children did mind, but we had no end of trouble with the teachers. That made us rather unpopular, but the real bother we had was when we went round collecting the dustbins in the early morning. It wasn't so much that the owners complained; the mistake was leaving them all in the free library. Not that anybody uses it, but the police objected. And we've more or less had to give up scavenging parties for the present. We could have an eloping party, of course."

Phyllis Morel clapped her hands. "An eloping party! That sounds heavenly. How does one do it?"

"I'm not sure. I was reading about one the other day, but it didn't give very full directions. I've never tried it; we should have to work it out for ourselves."

"Do let's have one to-morrow."

"If the weather holds. But it has to be done at night, of course, so we've lots of time to think over the arrangements."

Angela, at the other end of the table was congratulating Mr. Halliford on being rich enough to pretend to be a farmer. "I've always gathered from my friends that the only crab about farming is, you inevitably go bankrupt. Not to be in danger of going bankrupt, and being interested in all the oats and things that grow all over the place, must be perfect."

"I'm getting into the spirit of it," admitted Halliford. "But, you see, it's a kind of medicine; and medicine always tastes nasty at first."

"How do you mean, medicine?"

"Why, I've been bothered with nerves; and the doctors told me I must chuck up business and take to something quieter instead. I thought farming would be the next best thing; but, heaven help us, it's quiet."

"Don't you believe him, Mrs. Bredon," put in Carberry on her left. "It's the other way round; his nerves never began to go wrong until he started living quietly. Out in South Africa he hadn't anything wrong with his nerves. It's over here people go soft, when they've made their pile and have time to stop and think."

"*I* don't call it farming," said Mrs. Arnold, from his left. "Real farming means minding quite frightfully whether it rains to-morrow or not. Real farmers like Leslie are wanting rain now, but do you suppose Walter cares? He doesn't mind what happens to the roots. And of course, it's people like him, who have money to throw away, who are the ruin of English farming, with their silos and their tractors and all the rest of it. The real farmers can't get Government to pay any attention to

31

them. *Look at a man like Halliford*, they say ; HE'S *doing all right*."

It was at this moment that the ladies got up, and the great agrarian question was fortunately buried. " But if I were Mr. Halliford," Angela said to herself as she went out, " I would use my money to surround myself with people I liked and with people who liked me."

LIFE AT LASTBURY was not really comfortable ; even Angela, with all the anxiety good wives feel to prove that they have been in the right, could not pretend that it was. No room seemed to be devoted to any particular purpose ; none seemed conducive to any occupation except that of listening to gramophones. There were books, but they were the sort of books that lie about on tables with no dignified tenure of shelf-space ; there were meal-times, but nobody seemed to pay any attention to them ; there were flower beds, but they seemed to have been furnished by contract, the lobelia everywhere predominating. The pictures, the furniture, the food, were calculated to excite rather than to gratify the senses. Wherever you went, there was noise ; here a loudspeaker breathing out throaty inaccuracies about to-morrow's weather, there a gramophone, wallowing in the revolting eroticism of the American negro, and his still more revolting religiosity ; nor did anybody seem inclined to hush these noises as a prelude to conversation. Everybody behaved with the odd inconsistency of a society which has aped its manners ; bathed early in the morning and went back to breakfast in bed, or breakfasted in beach suits and then put on heavy tweeds to go out fishing. The servants were superior but incompetent, evidently from want of supervision ; the mainstay of the household was an elderly butler who had seen good service till recently and preserved, in that exile, the forlorn dignity of a piece of bankrupt stock. " Picnicking," Bredon called it, " on the ruins of an older civilisation " ; of that civilisation Cecil Worsley was an incongruous reminder, as he shambled about the place with his hands in his pockets, picking up a book here and there, burying himself in a review, or solemnly playing clock golf by himself on a fatally precipitous lawn.

Bredon, who had learned that the nearest golf-links were ten miles away, had not the moral courage to take refuge there on the first morning of his stay ; he had mentally put down Mrs. Halliford as the kind of hostess who would want to organise you and make you do something – in which he was quite wrong, for she did not appear till luncheon. He wandered out by himself, in the haze of a summer morning in which the sun has not yet found its strength, taking his geographical bearings, pursuing weed-grown paths by the river side, and finally coming out at the end of the drive through which they had approached the day before. Halliford was still engaged in silo-worship and introduced him with alacrity still further into those mysteries : made him look in through the hatches at the gaunt, cylindrical wall that towered up to the skylight, explained the precise point of juiciness at which your vetch and beans and oats were ripe for immurement, deafened him by continuing to shout in his ear when the chopping-machine set to work and made all other sounds inconspicuous. It was neither love of animals, nor kindness for his fellowman, but an imperious need of silence that made Bredon ask to be shown round the farm generally ; and for the rest of the morning he was exclaiming at the ingenuity of milk-testers, or standing in open doorways to return, with assumed confidence, the stare of truculent Herefordshire bulls.

At the luncheon table, conversation returned to an abandoned theme of the night before – the eloping party. " You *must* tell us more about it, Myrtle," urged Phyllis Morel. " I dreamt about it all last night. How do you arrange who's to elope with whom, and who wins, anyhow ? And is it all supposed to happen suddenly, or do you fix a zero hour ? It will be a perfect night for it to-night ; and

I'm not a bit certain when I may have to leave.
Do let's."

" I didn't read the thing very carefully,"
said Mrs. Halliford, " but as far as I remember
the point is for the eloping couple to get back
to the house without anybody knowing who
the man was. You appoint an arbitrary place
as ' Gretna Green,' and both hare and hounds
have to reach it by one route and come back by
another, arranged beforehand."

" I don't remember anything about guessing
who the man was." The interruption came
from Mrs. Arnold. " That's just like you,
Myrtle ; you always invent things. Have you
got that copy of the *Babbler* about still ? "

" No ; we send the old ones to the hospital.
I could have sworn I saw something about
secrecy, though. Perhaps you remember all
about it ? "

" Too many worries, I'm afraid, to remember
everything I read in the *Babbler*. You'd know,
Myrtle, if you had any children. But I'm perfectly certain the point was simply who could
make the best speed. Why, it stands to reason
you can't keep the names of the eloping parties
dark. How are they going to get away from
the company without everybody knowing
they've gone ? "

" We might wait till we've all gone to
bed."

"Even then, there'd be one wife and one husband who would know who was missing."

"Stop a bit," interrupted Mrs. Carberry, "couldn't we put that right? How would it be if we had a zero hour fixed and arranged that all the women should be in their rooms and all the men sitting up downstairs? Oh, but then the men would know who was missing, of course."

Bredon ventured on a suggestion. "Shouldn't we all be running into one another in the garage getting our cars out? And shouldn't we all notice who was there, and whose car was out already?"

"Oh, but we must have *some* surprise about it," objected Phyllis. "Couldn't we have all the cars drawn up in the drive? We shouldn't notice so much then."

"That would do," assented Mrs. Halliford. "And, look here, I know what. We'll have the Mossman at the head of the procession – it will be coming back any time now – and then Jack and I can use the Bridge. The hares, whoever they are, can use the Mossman; it's childishly easy to drive, and it ought to give them a good start."

"I wish we could have the guessing business, though," persisted Mrs. Carberry. "We might leave all the men behind, you know, except of course the eloper."

37

" What ! " cried her husband, " and have my little girl careering all over the countryside without me ? I know my little girl too well. No, I'm in on this, and if you're making the running you'll find me pretty close behind, my old angel."

Jack Carberry always created a moment of uncomfortable pause when he attempted the jocose. Tollard turned quickly to Angela and relieved it by breaking away from the particular to the general. " I suppose," he said, " the Victorians would have been rather shocked by all this."

" Just a little," admitted Angela. " But then of course they're dead. I sometimes wonder we spend so much time trying to shock people who aren't there."

" Well, let's get it fixed," suggested their host. " That is, if people would really like to do it. Anybody want to fall out ? What about you, Worsley ? No car."

" I've no car, as you say. If I am the lucky man, of course, politeness will turn me into acquiescent ballast. Otherwise, I have no objection to keeping the home refrigerators freezing. I've an article, really, I ought to be writing in any case."

" Personally, I'm all for staying at home," said Tollard, " I think the whole thing's rather rot. But I'll go if I'm wanted. By the way, if I'm the victim, my car drops out ; I've no one to drive it for me."

" Yes, that's true," agreed Halliford. " Still, let's hope it won't happen. You, Arnold ? "

" Well, I really think, unless I'm very badly wanted . . ."

" Nonsense," said his wife. " Of course I shall want you ; who's going to jack up the car if there's a puncture ? Unless, of course, you're with the hares – but then I needn't start. What about choosing the hares ? I think they drew lots, didn't they, in the article ? "

" I can't quite remember," said Mrs. Halliford, " whether they drew lots for both, or whether they drew lots for the women, and she chose her deliverer herself."

" Oh, that would be much better," Phyllis maintained. " She can let him know somehow in the course of the afternoon, without the rest of us spotting her. May I get down and covet some notepaper ? Then we can draw lots at once. Oh, and the damage ? We must have some money on it."

" Six cars, ain't we ? " said Halliford. " Let's make it a fiver all round to the hares, if they get away, and if they lose, a tenner to the hound who catches 'em. How would that do ? "

" If we really want to," put in his wife. " Mrs. Bredon, aren't you dreadfully tired after yesterday's drive ? I don't want to run people in for it if it bores them."

" Oh, we're on," said Angela. " When my husband makes faces like that across the table he is always trying to register cheery acquiescence. And next to winning twenty-five pounds I can't think of anything I should enjoy more than winning ten. We have car luck, you know, Mrs. Halliford, I often let my husband drive, and nothing seems to happen."

" Good ! Phyllis dear, do get one or two sheets of paper from the desk over there, and halve them down the middle. Let's see, we shall want five. . . . Thanks most awfully. Now, where's my pen ? I shall write E on one of them, standing for Eloper – or is it Eloperess ? Blast this pen, it never will write. Ah, that's better. This is what you've all got to pray for, my dears " – and she exhibited a large E written in the middle of the sheet. The sheets were folded and put into a vanity-bag that lay beside her, the bag was shut and given to Cecil Worsley to shake, then all the women drew solemnly in turn. " Keep your faces, please," said Mrs. Halliford as they drew ; " I can read you like a book, Phyllis, if you're not careful." (Angela declared afterwards that Miss Morel's face showed a tiny shadow of disappointment ; but it only went to prove, what Miles had always said, that Angela was fanciful.) "Remember you've got a detective here," she added, with an arch glance at the representative of the Indescribable.

"What does Myrtle mean by calling you a detective?" asked Worsley, as they went out to have coffee on the verandah. "I thought amateur detectives didn't exist in real life." And, when Miles had given his shamefaced explanation, "Ah, yes, it's a great company. I believe it stands to lose about five hundred pounds in the event of my premature decease. But I dare say they could stand that. I see you and I are the old-fashioned ones of the party, Mr. Bredon. But don't let's make the mistake of thinking the new generation frivolous because they take their jokes seriously." And he passed on into the garden.

Over coffee the conditions of the evening's entertainment were finally settled. They would dine early; they would not dress for dinner; the women would go to their rooms at half-past ten, the men sitting up downstairs until the alarm was given, but in different rooms. The cars were to be drawn up in a line in the drive, with the Mossman in front, dedicated to the service of the elopers. (It had already come back repaired, and stood now outside the front door – a huge touring car which looked as if it were meant for the needs of a large family, so wide were the seats, so ample the luggage-trunk at the back, so roomy its mysterious pockets, so elaborate its luxury fittings.) There was to be no fixed zero hour ; the heroine was to make her own arrangements with her chosen eloping-partner, and they were to leave together, from the front door, not earlier than half-past ten. The pursuers were to be delayed by having to leave at the drawing-room windows and make for the drive by a roundabout garden path. " Gretna Green " was to be a garage at King's Norton which was open all night ; if the hares reached it before any of the hounds drew level with them, they were the winners. The servants would be warned to keep indoors, so that there should be no danger of pedestrian traffic along the first lap, to the end of the drive. Wives to start without their husbands if they did not find them ready at the cars. Any driver was at liberty to take the Ledbury or the Bromyard road to Worcester as preferred. In the event of an accident, no stakes to be paid over.

Little was done that enervating afternoon, except that Mrs. Halliford went out to pay a brief call on a neighbour. At tea, Phyllis Morel announced that she would not have to leave, after all, till next week. " Is the post in already ? " asked Mrs. Arnold. Mrs. Halliford, it appeared, had picked it up on her way, and it was in the hall if anybody wanted it. Halliford volunteered to collect the whole array, and soon the party was indulging in that abstracted conversation which public letter-reading begets.

"What's that extraordinary-looking yellow communication, Walter?" asked his wife, seeing him knitting his brows over what looked like a superior kind of advertisement.

"Only a tout from a wine merchant."

"I got it too," said Worsley. "A really unique opportunity of buying Bechuanaland Tokay. Talking of unique opportunities, I trust the lady who is managing affairs to-night has selected her cavalier, or will select him soon. It is the waiting that is so trying."

"I wonder, Cecil, whether that means you've been picked already," suggested Mrs. Halliford.

"I won't be accused of bluff, at my age. Somebody had got to say that, so why not me? As a matter of fact, I don't see how that article will ever get written if I am to have an evening of excitements. But I intend to be inscrutable. The most penetrating of detectives shall not wrest my secret from me."

"I wish the most penetrating of detectives would wrest my pipe from somewhere," complained Halliford, rummaging about miserably in the search for it. "I wonder if I left it down at the silo? If so, it's probably got about two loads of mixed crop on the top of it by now."

"Don't be so restless, Walter," urged his

43

wife. " There's another pipe in your dressing-room ; I saw it only this morning ; you'd much better get that. Alexis, my angel, come here and have your finger dressed. He's cut it," she explained, " playing with something. Do you mind holding him, Walter ? He'll bite like sin."

IT WOULD BE idle to pretend that the consciousness of forthcoming adventure did not
cast a shadow over the earlier part of the evening.
They were festive outwardly: Mrs. Halliford
had put out crackers, which meant wearing
comic paper head-dresses, and had dealt out
little white "favours" all round, "So that we
shall recognise one another in the ditch," she
said, " or in the police court." But the evening
went slowly.

We are men tempered of base clay, not thinking machines. And grown-up people, no less
than children, are carried away by their own
illusions, once they give themselves up to the
spirit of make-believe. What else is fox-
hunting? The cynic's unfriendly description
of it as the "pursuit of the impossible after the
uneatable" may be logical enough, but the
thing goes on; some echo, perhaps, some race-
memory of earlier hunting, in dead earnest, stirs
in the blood and sweeps away hard-headed men
and women in the trail of its excitement. And
if, as Bredon suggested, our modern pastimes

lack that feudal dignity, if the intrusion of me-
chanism into our lives has made the return to
the primitive more difficult for us, we cherish our
illusions still. Everyone at Lastbury knew that
the event they expected was a deliberate sham :
a bogus elopement in which the thrill of sex
would play no part and no social usage would be
outraged. They knew, further, that the whole
element of secrecy and suddenness was extra-
neous to the affair, artificial and meaningless ;
there was nothing to it, really, but a cold-blooded
motor race along frequented roads at midnight.
But, perhaps because we never cease to be children, perhaps once more from some influence of
race-memory, the combination of hare and
hounds with blindman's-buff thrilled them with
anticipation and made the hours of waiting drag
heavily.

The whole party, you would say, had tacitly
conspired to put a poker face on the evening.
The women who had drawn blanks, the men
who had received no notice of an assignation –
and of these, let us make no secret about it, were
Miles and Angela – felt bound to " play up " by
looking inscrutable and ill at ease ; so only could
the general atmosphere of mystification be fos-
tered. If you caught somebody's eye by accident, you looked away guiltily, as if in fear that a
meaning glance might be intercepted. If you
found two people together you pretended to

suspect a *tête-à-tête* ; if you found one alone you backed out of the room to avoid the imputation of it. On their side the elopers, whoever they were, kept up their imposture admirably ; nobody could be set down as betraying just too much or just too little of agitation. The only person who insisted on playing with fire was the person least likely to be involved in the proceedings at all, Cecil Worsley ; he was continually hazarding guesses, making innuendoes, speculating on possible evasions of the by-laws.

Then, an hour or so after dinner, he got up suddenly and left the room with one of his abrupt gestures, as a grown-up person will who has long been playing with the children, and suddenly remembered the imperious necessity of a smoke.

As the evening wore on the suspense grew heavier. Ordnance maps were passed from hand to hand, notes exchanged as to the gradients of the Malverns, as to the possibility of interference by officious police. At twenty minutes past ten Mrs. Halliford, who seemed to be infected by now with the general restlessness, began to wonder whether the drive gate was open ? If it was shut the elopers would evidently be placed under an immediate handicap. Nobody could remember, so her husband was despatched to walk up the drive and make sure.

" And when you come back, go to your study ;
we must keep the men separate." At last the
half hour struck, and the whole party converged
on the front door, to take a final look at the
weather before they dispersed to their rooms.
The night was clear, though the moon was
clouded, and the colour of the bushes showed up
in the strong light that flooded out from the
porch. Though the other cars had been moved
off to their allotted stations, the Mossman was
still there, a huge shadow blocking the entrance ;
its mascot at one end, its luggage-trunk at the
other, reproduced in fantastic shadows on the
leaves opposite.

" I'll just take it up to the head of the column," said Mrs. Halliford, " and I may as well
see what Walter's doing ; he ought to be back by
now." They heard the scrunching of the wheels
on the gravel, then quiet again as she passed
through the gate, which was evidently open, and
halted there. The gaunt shape of the silo was
flood-lighted for a moment as she passed it.
Then there were cries of " Walter, Walter ! "
six or seven times repeated, but no answering
shout. The car moved on some thirty or forty
feet, and there were fresh, rather fainter repeti-
tions of the name. Then the car was put into
reverse, and the silo was illuminated again. " It
doesn't matter," explained Mrs. Halliford as she
came back to them ; " I expect he's gone down

by the river path ; he'll be in in a minute. That path, remember, and the french windows at the back are the way the hounds get to their cars ; the hares must have the front door to themselves, or they won't be able to make their getaway. Now, off to your stations, and don't fall asleep. Make straight for the cars when you see the first couple leave. No good-nights, yet, but good hunting, everybody." And she ushered the women upstairs to the rooms appointed for them ; the men collected drinks and took up their separate quarters on the ground floor.

Each member of the party was now looking out, in solitude, on the front of the house; which meant that almost all the front windows were illuminated, and cast vivid squares of light on the drive or on the grass lawn just beyond it. Thus each saw all the others in silhouette ; you would have thought, indeed, that you were looking out at a silhouette show on a life-size scale. They disappeared and reappeared at intervals, as if to keep the mystification going. Bredon was in a small room close to the main door ; immediately above him was a figure smoking a phantom cigarette – Mrs. Halliford, he realised, for he heard her singing a little. He recognised, even at a distance, Angela's profile – he had long been word perfect in it, but the others confused him, and he tortured himself, as he waited, with the effort to get them sorted out. There was no doubt about Carberry, just the other side of the front door. He was still wearing a fool's cap, out of a cracker ; how enormous it looked ! Worsley, of course, would not be looking out, for he would not hunt with the hounds in any case . . . was that Tollard, or was it Arnold, at the further end ? Anyhow there were the two of them, and . . . yes, that fresh light must mean that Halliford had come in ; a full house. The shadows from the upper windows were too distorted by perspective to be worth conjecture. . . . Time seemed to be slipping away ; that pipe was nearly full when the women went upstairs, and here he was knocking it out. Yes, the elopers were taking their time. Hullo, Angela's shadow had gone ; could she possibly . . . ? Oh, confound it ! No, she was back at her window again. A moment later, and two lights disappeared almost simultaneously. By Gad, Mr. and Mrs. Halliford ! An unadventurous choice, surely, for such a woman. Yes, there they were at the front door ; they had switched the light off, but there was no mistaking those two figures. Now, where was that electric torch ? Full speed ahead for the garden path.

He thought he had made good time, but Angela was there ahead of him in the driver's seat. This was annoying, for they had arranged that whoever climbed in first was to do the driving ; and Bredon, like most men, was convinced that his wife's driving was criminally dangerous. " Well, you might say *Thank God* or something," she pointed out as she switched on the lights. " Weren't you expecting to have me careering all over the countryside with old Pa Carberry ? How absurd it is to feel all worked up like this ! Somebody got away ahead of us ; did you see who it was ? Oh, the Morel girl ; of course, she hadn't to wait for anybody."

" If that's an insult, it's uncalled for. I was never quicker off the mark, though I would have you observe that I was lighting a pipe at the time. I think it's very lucky we weren't ahead ; if you hadn't that rear light to steer by you'd have had me in the ditch by now, and you will yet."

" Rot, we're hardly moving. Wait till we get into that main road, and you'll see sights. I say, Mrs. H. must have had a nasty quarter of an hour when she thought her eloping-partner had walked out on her. No wonder she went shouting *Walter* all over the place."

" Ye-es."

" Are you being inscrutable ? I can't see in this light."

51

"Not very. I was only thinking it was rather rum that she should have made off with her own husband ; shouldn't have thought that was her idea of a large evening."

"Suppose she thought he'd pile up the other car if she left him to drive it alone. Some husbands . . ."

"Talk less and change the gears a trifle sooner. You'll have the guts out of her."

There was no doubt about the thrill of this midnight chase, though it was all "pretend," and Bredon's car had before now taken the road at this pace on sterner errands. Shadows of haystacks, of cattle in the hedges, loomed enormous ; startled rabbits made the pace for a few yards, and disappeared at the last moment into the long grass ; late-retiring householders looked out, in angry *décolleté*, from their windows ; straggling villages seemed interminable in the dark. There was no difficulty about finding the way ; the red rear light of the car in front never drew ahead, yet never did they look like overhauling it. When they were well into Hereford, it stopped suddenly ; and Angela prudently reduced her speed to a minimum ; she looked like one taking out a maiden aunt for carriage exercise when she passed, at a crossroads, Phyllis Morel having trouble with the police. "This puts us on velvet," she commented. "Now, which is it

to be, Bromyard or Ledbury? Ledbury?
Perhaps you're right ; it's something to have
been over the road before." There was more
traffic now to be reckoned with ; there were
loose-jointed lorries that always seemed about
to lurch across the road at the wrong moment,
there were fast cars going their own way, which
they overhauled breathlessly, and recognised
with disappointment as nothing like the Mossman. The Malvern Hills, even so late, were
dotted with mysterious lights (every town
seems four times its size by lamplight), but
there seemed to be no policemen here to interfere
with the chase either way. At last, well after
midnight, they were down in the plain of Severn,
and finished breathlessly, the last few miles into
Worcester. From Worcester to King's Norton
traffic was commoner, and the pace slower.
The all-night garage was easily found, easily
recognised by the couple who stood in front of
it. " Oh, there you are ! " said Mrs. Halliford.
" The blacksmith has just gone in to put his
prayer-book away."

Within twenty minutes, they were joined
by the Arnolds, who had made the distance
through Bromyard, and the Carberrys, who
reported that Tollard was not to be expected ;
they had passed him, hardly a mile out from
Lastbury, apparently broken down. The way
back, it must be confessed, was something of

an anticlimax ; Bredon drove, and Angela slept continuously beside him. They had gone upstairs before Mrs. Halliford came in from putting the Mossman into its garage.

AFTER A LATE night, whatever the excuse for it, we all feel that we have a right to a long lie. And Bredon was justly indignant when, still heavy with sleep, he was awoken by the discreet tapping of a maidservant and found his watch registering a quarter past six. Mr. Halliford's apologies for disturbing him, but he would like to see him, if he might, on an urgent matter.

Walter Halliford was in the passage, his face drawn and white, his clothes hastily thrown on, the picture of discomposure. " I'm most awfully sorry, but I'm afraid a rather terrible thing has happened. Cecil Worsley . . ."

" Gone sick ? "

" Dead. Out there in the silo. Can't make it out at all. The workmen came and told me about it ; I've just been down. I've phoned for the doctor, but I didn't like to call in the police till he's been. Only I thought perhaps you were accustomed to this sort of thing and wouldn't mind coming down to have a look round first."

" Rather not. I'm no sort of use, though. The doctor will tell you to get the police, sure to.

55

I'll just put on one or two things, then I'm with you. I'm most awfully sorry about this."

Those who are accustomed to have their lives managed for them by servants find a great horror of loneliness in a house seen at an early hour of the morning when the rooms have not been " done." There is a strange petrifaction of yesterday's experience – your glass standing where you left it, cards lying about still unmade, books and newspapers still open, cushions sprawling anyhow, the grate full of spent matches, the daylight filtering in through half-closed curtains, and over all a desolate smell of stale tobacco. Conscience may tell you that in fact you passed an uncommonly quiet evening, but there is a scruple which bids you hold yourself responsible for all this unfamiliar disarray. At that raw hour in the morning tragic news is, in any case, stultifying enough ; this atmosphere of desolation superadded to it is almost unbearable ; " here," you say to yourself, " he sat yesterday ; the cushions are still crumpled with the imprint of his form." Bolts rattle, and the key turns reluctantly in the lock, as if preparing to disclose a guilty secret. Nor, that day, did the outer air belie the impressions communicated indoors. It was none of your bright mornings, full of sunshine and cockcrow and fresh smells of earth. The heat had brought up a heavy dew, which wreathed the garden in fantastic shapes of mist ; the opposite bank of the river showed faint and unsubstantial, the air was breathless, still charged with heat, but unpropitious to clean thoughts and the melody of birds. They went out as if into an evil fairyland.

" Too awful," Halliford was saying. " Such a good fellow, and a very old friend of Myrtle's. I had to tell her, and she's badly knocked out by it. What makes it worse is, one can't be certain the poor fellow didn't take his own life. Been working very hard, you know, lately, over Government business ; told us he wanted to come down here to get a complete rest. We'd never forgive ourselves, Myrtle and I, if we felt that a little more care and attention might have saved him from this."

" Suicide ? " asked Bredon. " It's a queer case of it, if so. I mean, you say the gases that come off a silo can easily make a man pass out suddenly, and I suppose painlessly. But is it certain they will do it every time ? And did Worsley know that ? I should have thought a good deep river close by would look the easiest way out."

" I know. But, come to think of it, an accident like that is a queer kind of accident ; considering the man, considering the time of day. Here we are, look for yourself."

They had now reached the drive gate, and

were aware of a melancholy group contemplating the silo. The farm hands, unable to go on with their work for fear of tampering with the scene of the tragedy, were standing idly about, adducing, in high Welsh-English, a score of gruesome parallels. " That's the easiest way to look in," suggested Halliford, pointing to a set of iron stanchions by which you could climb up facing the hatches. These hatches, it should be explained, are successively closed as the silage is heaped up, to prevent any air reaching it from the side. The lowest three, therefore, were closed ; when Bredon's face was on a level with the fourth he could see, when it was on a level with the fifth he could get a clear view of the scene within. It was, indeed, an uncertain light, curtained with mist and filtering down from the skylight at the top – the hatches themselves, for some reason which was obscure to him, were sheltered from the light by a kind of wooden chimney, jutting out behind the stanchions on which he was climbing. It gave a solemn effect – by false analogy, you imagined, with the light that comes from the clerestory of a cathedral. There was no need, however, of adventitious solemnity here ; the dark form which lay hunched up in the middle of the silage was enough to secure that.

" Is it all right to go in ? " Bredon shouted back to his host.

" Yes, but for the Lord's sake don't stay long. There may be some gas about still, and there's hardly any ventilation. Just have a look at him and come back."

There was no difficulty, Bredon observed, in letting yourself in through the open hatch. A man like Worsley, slight of build but wiry, would have found it easy enough. There was, though, something about the unnatural way in which the body was hunched up which suggested, rather, the idea that the dead man might have climbed the ladder outside and fallen, or thrown himself, through the skylight. It was neither, you felt, the position in which a man falls when he faints suddenly, nor the position in which a man would lie down to compose himself for his last sleep. The face, too, when he lifted it gently from where it lay half buried in the silage, suggested to him the horror of a foreseen danger. But he was no expert in such symptoms, and he left the discussion of them to the doctor when he should come. Worsley had been dressed in his day clothes and in tennis-shoes – they had none of them dressed for dinner last night – and the only sign of disarray about them was that the collar had come loose, or been torn loose, breaking off the head of the stud. There had been a fall, then, it seemed, or else a last struggle for breath. There had been a slight cut on the forefinger of the right hand, which had bled a little. There was a very small tear on the right shoulder of the coat ; but this might have happened at any time ; Worsley was not a very careful man about his clothes. . . . Nothing else to be seen, apparently ; it was no business of his to search the pockets ; he had best get back into the fresh air. Hullo, what was that he had knocked his foot against ? A briar pipe ; better take that out with him, after marking carefully where it lay.

" Where did you get that ? " asked Halliford as he climbed out. " It's mine ; couldn't find it all yesterday evening. Did I drop it in the silo ? I was there in the afternoon, of course."

" Must have," assented Bredon. " It was just there, a bit over a yard from the hatches. I had imagined for the moment it might be his. Did he smoke ? I can't remember."

" Very seldom ; and not a pipe. Cigarettes when he was fishing, and very rarely a cigar after dinner. I suppose better not look in his pockets, in case we should have the police about. Hullo, here's the doctor."

A young, rather serious-looking man was approaching them from the small runabout car in which he had driven up. We are all in two minds whether we would prefer a doctor, at moments of crisis, to register human sympathy or professional competence. In this one, professional competence was the prevailing note, though he wore the appropriate air of respectful concern. The name of Worsley meant nothing to him ; for him, the dead man was just a guest at a house-party. His tour of inspection was much like Bredon's and produced little more result.

" You didn't try to take him out ? " he said.

" I didn't see the use," explained Halliford. " I was a stretcher-bearer in the War, and I know a dead man all right when I see one. Could the men have done anything when they first found him ? "

" Nothing at all. He's been dead for hours. Since midnight at least. Much best to leave him and let the police have a look at him, to avoid any unpleasantness later on. What time did your men find him ? "

" Just after six, sir," said one of them, clearly anxious to get his tale told. " We're working early hours now, see, because you must fill the silo when the crop is right. John Hookway went up by the ladder to open the trap, and, *Oh God !* he said, *what's that in there ?* Then I looked in through the hatches, and I sent him up to the house to fetch Mr. Halliford. I thought if we went in, look, we should be all dead men too."

" What time did you knock off last night ? " asked the doctor.

" Five o'clock, sir, because there was no more of the crop yet to carry. There was never nobody near the place in the afternoon, none of the gentlemen, except Mr. Halliford."

" M'yes. That gives plenty of time for the gas to form. You ought to keep this place locked up, Mr. Halliford, when they aren't working. I suppose he just looked in and thought he would like to explore the place, and then the fumes caught him suddenly. No reason, I suppose, to think – you'll excuse my asking . . ."

" How do I know, doctor ? " protested Halliford. " He had been a good deal run down, as I was telling Mr. Bredon here just now ; but he seemed in very good spirits last night – wouldn't you say that ? "

" Excellent," admitted Bredon. " If there was any question of suicide, it must have been a sudden inspiration – or else he was acting incredibly well all last night. Just before he went off to do some work, he was telling us that he was going to wait till we had all gone and lock up the monkey in somebody's bedroom, only he wouldn't tell us whose. That *couldn't* be acting."

This mention of the previous evening involved explanations for the benefit of the doctor ; embarrassed explanations, for we are ashamed, at such times, of our dead frivolities. The doctor strongly urged calling in the police at once. " It would have been different if there had been anybody in the house, or if anybody had seen the unfortunate fellow a little time before his death. But, with the house empty like that, you can't be answerable for what went on."

"All right ; I'll ring them up now. Coming in for some breakfast ? They'll want you, I suppose."

"Thanks very much, but I've got rather an interesting case under observation at the hospital ; I think I'll get back. If you'll just give me a ring when the police are here, I can come over and make a proper autopsy. Not that there's any sort of doubt here."

"Just poisoning from the silo ? "

"Call it poisoning if you like, suffocation if you like. The fumes off that stuff are just carbonic acid gas ; in plain English, fug. Want of oxygen, that's what he died of, poor chap. They're rare, these cases ; but there's nothing complicated about them."

And he started up his car and, with a wave of the hand, was gone.

CHAPTER VII : THE GARDEN BEFORE BREAKFAST

BREDON EXCUSED HIMSELF from accompanying his host when he went back to telephone. He felt, he said, rather sickened by the morning's experience and by the close atmosphere of the silo ; he would walk about a bit and get some fresh air before breakfast. His real reason was quite different ; he wanted to have a look round while the ground was still fresh. He was of all men the least inclined to feel, or to obey, those unaccountable premonitions which convince people – or so they say afterwards – that "something is wrong." An accident, a suicide, why not ? Accidents and suicides happened every day. But there would be no harm in trying to trace, if any traces were left, the steps which led up to the tragedy ; and besides . . . "coincidences do happen," he reminded himself, "but one doesn't like to find too many of them all lying about together."

There were two ways from the front door of

Lastbury to the drive gate and to the silo which stood by it. One was along the drive itself, the way they had come. But the drive, following the line of the contours to avoid dipping, curved before it reached the gate ; curved round the end of a walled garden, full of strawberry beds, asparagus, cucumber-frames and fruit trees. The direct way to the house, then, was the path down the centre of this garden ; but, as there was an iron gate at each end of it and you were liable to find either locked, it was always doubtful whether you would save time by adopting the alternative. It was just possible, though, that a man strolling about idly late in the evening would saunter in here ; just possible that a man determined to make away with himself might slink down such a path, eager to avoid all possibility of human encounter. Yes, it was worth trying the garden path and seeing if it had any story to tell of last night.

" Not," Bredon pointed out to himself, " that there is really the least likelihood of any traces being left at all. Here you have a perfectly fine evening, after several days of drought, so that there is no mud on the pathways ; you have a man (presumably) walking unmolested in a place where he knows his way about perfectly well, a non-smoker, or practically so ; it is dark, so there is no temptation to wander about over flower-beds. No, it will be the hundredth chance if he has left his mark about." The gate, he found, was open – by the way, was not the openness of the gate itself an oddity ? These iron gates were sometimes open by day, presumably because gardeners were going to and fro ; but they were not *always* open ; and surely a gate that is sometimes shut is certain to be shut at night ? Lastbury was a lonely place, but presumably it had youthful inhabitants capable of a raid on gooseberry bushes. Now, if Halliford had opened the gate that morning, why had he not chosen that route when they went down to the silo together ? Only yesterday, in argument, he had been maintaining that it was a shorter journey. Could Worsley have opened it last night ? But then, when you come to think of it, it was unlikely that he would have taken the trouble to get a key, even if he knew where the keys were left. No, that fact must simply be docketed in the mind, not underlined as important ; meanwhile, it would be as well to leave the gate just as he found it, about an inch open ; he must be careful, because it locked automatically – there, that would do.

He turned round, to find a half-smoked cigar almost at his feet. Once more, did that mean anything ? Had Worsley smoked a cigar after dinner the night before ? It was too childish that one couldn't remember things like that. And yet, if one remembered everything important and unimportant one would go mad, like Coleridge's man on the top of St. Paul's. He could remember Carberry smoking a cigar, and Halliford himself of course ; Tollard ? No, Tollard was smoking a pipe, because he had trouble with it when it refused to draw. About Arnold and Worsley, he decided, he had no memories whatever. Then he saw that he was being a fool ; this cigar could not be one smoked immediately after dinner in any case. It must either be one Worsley had lit – to steady himself, perhaps – when he went out, close on midnight ; or it was one Halliford had dropped, after luncheon, say. Halliford was always pottering down to the silo. You cannot date a cigar that has, in any case, spent several hours in the open.

As he looked up from the cigar – he had not touched it – his eye lit on a maximum-and-minimum thermometer, with a magnet clumsily attached to it, evidently for the purpose of pulling the metal register back from maximum and minimum to reunite it with the mercury. No human being can pass a thermometer without reading it if he knows how. Bredon read it ; noticed that the temperature at the moment was 68, that it had been down as low as 59 during the night – and yesterday's maximum ? There was no record of yesterday's maximum ; the index was close to the mercury, ready to be pushed up. Now, that meant – let's see, that meant that the thermometer had been " set " some time since the great heat of yesterday afternoon ; since tea-time, you could say with fair certainty. Was it a gardener's job, he wondered, to do that sort of thing ? A magnet was just the sort of thing which would preserve fingerprints ; what about carrying it off with him ? Then he pulled himself together ; after all, this was not his show. Time enough to do lampblack experiments when the Indescribable started getting worried over that claim of five hundred on Worsley's life.

" Shouldn't wonder if they did, though," he commented to himself ; " they're terribly keen on being thorough." Meanwhile, it was clear that somebody had been through the walled garden since tea-time. But it was not, after all, very likely that this visit had been paid late at night. The sky had been over-clouded, and the visibility low ; you might have thought it the night for a stroll, but you would hardly have stood about striking matches with one hand and manipulating a magnet with the other, to make sure of to-morrow's temperature. No, if there was any significance in the facts he had noted hitherto, it was still difficult to connect them with Worsley's movements during, or just before, the eloping race.

He went on down the central path, looking anxiously on this side and that for the marks of some false step in the dark which might be registered on the soft earth of the beds. He found no footprints, but in looking for them he caught sight of something no less interesting – a paper cap, of the cracker variety, looking rather like what Napoleon might have worn at Waterloo if his tastes had run to light green and mauve. This, evidently, was much more like business. It lay perhaps a couple of feet from the edge of the path ; and, since the air had been so windless, it was reasonable to suppose that it lay where it fell. You could imagine Worsley, then, getting tired of writing his article, and deciding to take a turn outside ; finding the nearer garden gate open and sauntering up the central path. Half way along it, perhaps the scent of some flower arrests him in the darkness, and the absurd paper decoration slips off his head, unnoticed or unregretted. In the alternative, you could imagine him deliberately making his way to the silo, resolved on ending it all ; he puts up his hand to his forehead, as if to sweep away the clouds that hang over his brain, and, in doing so, touches with his fingers the incongruous paper crown, now serving as a fillet

for the victim ; he tosses it away impatiently.
. . . Odd, how easy it was to wear one of
those caps, and forget that you were wearing
it.

Well, that fixed his suspicion ; Worsley had
evidently gone out through the garden. Would
he be able to swear to that, at the inquest ?
Once again he reflected on the ludicrous inadequacy of human testimony. He knew that
Worsley had worn a paper cap overnight, but
the shape and shade of it eluded memory ;
asked offhand he would have said there was
pink about it. He could remember Carberry's
peaked affair, because it looked so fantastic
when reproduced by his shadow on the lawn.
He could remember his own Scots bonnet and
the light blue crown that suited Angela so when
she wore it. The rest simply would not come ;
there had been more crackers, and consequently
more caps, than people ; Mrs. Halliford had
insisted on exchanging head-dresses with her
husband ; nothing else known. Well, his early
prowl had not been altogether unrewarded ;
he had better be getting back to breakfast. The
gate at the other end of the garden looked as
if were open too.

And here was a further point, though of
course a very uncertain one – wouldn't Worsley
have crumpled up the paper cap and put it in
his pocket, instead of throwing it away untidily

in a flower-garden, if he had merely gone out
to take the air ?   Was it not more natural, this
time, to imagine him throwing it away impatiently, as a gay intrusion on his dark
thoughts ?   Well, that was only a long shot.
Meanwhile, Worsley *must* have been in the
garden.   Or was there some much deeper
explanation of the whole thing ?   " Heavens,"
he thought, " I am becoming a detective ! "
Breakfast, now, and less puzzling of the brain.
A man's first duty, after all, was to his diges-
tion.

The party which had dined under conditions
of spurious excitement was breakfasting late,
looking like a set of mutes.   The household was
so thoroughly disorganised that nobody, except
the hostess, had had the heart to demand breakfast in bed ; otherwise they would have avoided
the embarrassment of such a public meeting.
Mrs. Carberry alone, who had a kind of
boisterous honesty that could not tolerate
false decorum, kept a kind of conversation
going by referring, pitilessly, to the subject
that was in all their minds.   " I think it's awful
for you," she said to her host, " and worse for
Mrs. Halliford ; but for God's sake let's talk
about it or we shall go out of our minds.   Also,
if we don't discuss the thing rationally while
we're together, we shall all tell different lies,
quite unintentionally, to the police."

" I think that's true," said Phyllis. " It feels rather like cheating, but I'm so unnerved after my cross-questioning last night by that man in Hereford that I shall go all to pieces if I'm not careful. For heaven's sake remember, somebody, when it was that poor Mr. Worsley went out of the room. I know it was after the nine o'clock news bulletin, because he was talking about that. Can anybody get it more exact ? "

" I can," said Angela. " I can remember when the man brought in the whisky wondering whether it was Mr. Worsley coming back again. So he must have been gone some little time, I should say."

" That's luck," observed Mrs. Carberry. " Walter, what time do they bring the whisky in ? "

" Ten o'clock. Riddell is never late."

" Then that fixes it between, say a quarter past nine and a quarter to ten. During the time between that and the start for the race, we were all in the drawing-room, looking out on the river side of the house ; so that he may have gone out into the drive at any time while we assumed that he was upstairs writing his article. After that, we should have been bound to see him if he left by the front, though we should have missed him if he'd gone down the path by the river. Once we'd left, and that would be about eleven, he had the whole place to himself."

" *Cave*, old girl," Carberry put in suddenly. " There's someone driving up in front, and it looks to me a good deal like the police."

" I NEVER KNEW such a man," complained Angela. " First you kick like a mule about coming here ; and then, when you are here, nothing will dislodge you, even when your fellow-guests start dying all over the place."

Breakfast was over, and the married couples had crept away singly to discuss the question of the moment – Does one go or stay in a house which sudden death has turned into a house of mourning, when it is quite certain that there will be an inquest, and almost certain that you will be called on to give evidence at it ? Angela's point was that they hadn't any evidence to give beyond what could be given by any dog or cat in the house, and meanwhile common decency demanded that you should pack up. Halliford was with the police, and Mrs. Halliford had not yet put in an appearance ; so the moment was propitious for such discussions.

" No, honestly," said Miles, " you can go home if you like, but I simply must stop on here a bit, if there's any excuse for it – and I should say the inquest ought to be a good enough excuse. For one thing, Worsley was insured, though only for a ridiculous sum, and you know what the Indescribable are, how they boggle about pennies. They would never forgive me if I lost this heaven-sent chance of being their representative. And for another thing – well, if you must know, I'm not quite happy about this show, somehow."

" Happy? How do you mean? I didn't suppose anybody was, personally."

" I mean that the whole setting of last night was just a little too good to be true. God knows it's not a thing to chat to the police about ; I haven't a particle of evidence. But I feel there's been dirty work about somewhere ; that's the long and short of it."

" Mmm – you don't ordinarily get hold of mares' nests, Miles. I didn't realise your professional instincts were aroused ; I thought it was just morbid curiosity. Come on, then, let's have it ; it may be your last chance of getting my invaluable help for some little time to come. What's worrying you? "

" Why, the whole blasted thing. Look here, do you really think it was an accident? It was a dark night ; a man going out for a walk in the garden doesn't take an electric torch out with him, and as he wasn't really a smoker he probably hadn't even matches with him. Now, what was there about the silo that invited exploration in pitch darkness, when he could have explored it any time he wanted to ? If he climbed in, what made him climb in ? And if he fell in, why didn't he walk straight to the hatches at the side and climb out, instead of waiting about to be spifflicated ? Things like that will do for a jury, only out to defend a man from the charge of suicide. But if you are out to get the real truth, you don't want bare possibility, you want something probable ; some ordinary human motive."

" Yes, I think that's true. Of course, the poor man seemed to me a bit of a schoolboy ; bachelors like that often are. But I don't think he was quite schoolboy enough to want to climb about when he was by himself. It's partly a pose, that youthfulness of his, and he had nobody to pose to, down there at the silo. I don't really think he got in there for fun, or by mere accident. Well then ? "

" Suicide's a difficult thing to argue about ; one's no personal experience to go by. And it's certainly true that people indulge in odd forms of it. But, you know, there's this to be considered. Your suicide usually has time to think what's he's going to do and how he's going to do it. Not, of course, if he's running away from justice or from public scorn ; but the kind of suicide who just suffers from depression and finds life too much for him. Well,

Worsley was a nice man and superabundantly a gentleman, and the Hallifords were his friends. Do you think a man like that is going to borrow his friend's silo to commit suicide in without so much as a by your leave ? He wouldn't do it."

" Unless something came over him all of a sudden."

" In which case, ten to one, he'd have thrown himself into the river. A good deep river like that is a positive invitation to suicide, like looking over the edge of a cliff ; a silo isn't. Then here's another point – if he was contemplating suicide in any case, why didn't he announce his intention of staying at home whatever happened ? Instead of agreeing, as he did, to play hare if he were chosen for the job."

" Same criticism. Seldom the time and the place, and all that. You know what a gush of loneliness comes over one when everybody else has suddenly left a house which was chock full a quarter of an hour ago. That might just bring it on, make the depression acute."

" Yes, I suppose that's true. But even so, the silo ! Worsley never seemed to take any interest in the thing ; was it likely he knew the fumes were going to be fatal ? And, hang it all, how could he be certain they would be ? One knows they sometimes are, but nobody knows quite when or quite why. The suicide, whatever else he does, wants to make certain of the job. A pretty good fool he'd have looked if he'd woken up on a great pile of vetch and stuff with a slight headache.''

" That's the real crab ; I believe much more in that argument than the others. But, my precious, don't you see that it cuts both ways ? You want me to believe there's been a murder, don't you ? Well, if a suicide wants to make certain of the job, a murderer wants it much worse. He doesn't want his victim to wake up with a slight headache, does he ? And on your own showing he couldn't be certain that poor Worsley wouldn't.''

" Ah, but, you see, you're trying to pin me down to something positive. I don't know what happened, and I don't pretend to know what happened. He may have been suffocated somewhere else, and the body may have been parked in the silo for convenience. Or he may have been shut up in the silo for a joke, or for a bet, or by way of kidnapping, and the death may have been unforeseen. Or, for that matter, he may have been smothered under the silage, and dug out afterwards. All I say is, that somebody else had a hand in it ; it can't have been a one man show ; and that somebody hasn't thrown any light on the situation yet. That's what worries me ; that's why I'm going to stay here until I'm turned out.''

" That's a thing that never occurred to me ;

could he have been imprisoned in the silo, and got suffocated in the end only because it was impossible for him to scramble out ? "

" Yes, but only on the assumption, as I say, that there is dirty work about. You can climb out of the silo by the hatches, as long as they remain open ; they form a kind of natural ladder. And all the hatches above the level of the crop are left open in the ordinary way. But if somebody wants to imprison you in a silo, all he has got to do is to shut the hatches the whole way up. You can't climb up them then, because their framework doesn't jut out enough to give you foothold or handhold."

" But, Miles, it's all rather negative, isn't it ? You don't suspect anybody ; you simply don't see how to explain what happened except as the result, let's say, of violence ? "

" Oh, but I do suspect."

" Whom ? "

" I wish I knew ; person or persons unknown. Look here, I hate paying compliments, but you have always seemed to me a woman of average intelligence. Do you mean to say you think it was just a coincidence that the death of Cecil Worsley happened just at the moment when the household in which he was staying was scattered all over the countryside, playing this ridiculous eloping game ? Why, all the time I felt the eloping game was too good to be true. There

79

was something fantastic about it ; something which was all too obviously meant to be a blind. I wish I'd got up and said so at the time. But one never does ; one hangs on and hopes the thing will get clearer as it goes on."

" But the eloping game is all right, isn't it ? They found it in a back number of the *Gabbler*."

" Oh, yes, I suppose it's a perfectly genuine form of idiocy, not worse than many you get nowadays. That's true, and I suppose it's true that one always imagines *afterwards* that there was something wrong about the proceedings all the time, when the result is a tragedy. But tell me, honestly, didn't you feel that eloping game was being *forced* on us, much as you have a card forced on you by a conjuror ? "

" Did I ? I shall never be able to tell now, because you've suggested it to me. I think the only thing which seemed to me odd was the choice of hares ; we drew lots for the heroine, and she elected her own cavalier, and the result was that our host and hostess ran away from us, while the house-party scattered in pursuit. But I didn't think that worse than a coincidence."

" Well, and was it ? Not very odd that Mrs. Halliford should have drawn the lot ; she had a twenty per cent. chance. Not very odd that she should have chosen her husband, really ; it kept the whole twenty-five pounds in the family.

By the way, I suppose we ought to pay up that fiver. No, if you come to think of it it is the hounds who fall under suspicion of playing a crooked game, not the hares. The hares have to trek across the countryside from the word Go ; the hounds – well, nobody is in a position to say where this one or that one was at any given moment ; whether this one or that one really left the house at all, or how soon they left it."

" Oo, yes, that's more like it. But how do we set about guessing ? "

" Why, the obvious question to ask is, Who was it proposed playing that idiotic game ? Or anyhow, who insisted on it ? "

" This is terribly exciting. No doubt whatever, Miles, that you proposed it ; I heard you myself. I suppose Worsley hadn't paid up his last premium, and the Indescribable paid you to do him in while he was uninsured ? "

" Don't rag, woman ; this is serious. No, I talked about scavenging parties and gave the subject a lead. But it was Mrs. Halliford who first mentioned the eloping party. On the other hand, I don't know that she seemed very keen on it. It was Miss Morel, wasn't it, who kept on saying we must do it ? "

" Yes, but then, she would. She was also keen, if I remember right, about the parties remaining unknown till the last moment. Was that important ? I'm not quite clear what the advantage of the game is supposed to be from the criminal's point of view."

" I should have thought that was obvious. The game manufactured a quite unreal situation : for half an hour we were all of us watching the front of the house, so that anybody who left that way must be noticed, whereas anybody who left any other way couldn't be noticed. Then for ten minutes or so we were all rushing all over the place, nobody taking any notice of what his neighbour did. Then for the best part of three hours we were scattered over the countryside, so that anybody who liked to turn back halfway and come back to the house could do it without being spotted. Surely all that is a godsend to the criminal who wants to do his job unnoticed and then frame up an alibi on the top of it. No, I can't believe it's coincidence ; it's simply too good to be true."

" Mrs. Carberry, now I come to think of it, was pretty keen on the guessing business. And of course, she'd less reason to be keen on the game than Phyllis Morel."

" Why less reason ? "

" Oh, well, a child could see that Phyllis Morel is terribly in love with Tollard, and that he isn't sure whether he's in love with her or not. A female child, I mean ; men never notice anything. And of course, if Phyllis had drawn the lot she could have chosen Tollard to elope with, and, with a chance like that . . ."

"Angela, I despair of your sex. Let us hear no more of it. Still, as you say, Mrs. Carberry was rather keen that we shouldn't know beforehand who the eloping parties were. Mrs. Arnold wasn't."

"I don't know that Mrs. Arnold was very keen on the whole thing. I'm certain *he* wasn't. But the only person who really wanted to turn the whole system down was Mr. Tollard."

"Confound it all, when a subject like that is on the *tapis* it's quite impossible to remember who did really force the card. But one thing I'm certain of . . ."

He was interrupted by a knock at the door and an intimation that " the gentlemen from Hereford " would be obliged if Mr. Bredon could make it convenient to see them now. The vocabulary of the servants' hall, not being designed for emergencies, has no proper equivalent for the word " police."

THE GENTLEMEN FROM Hereford were evidently
embarrassed by having to interview such a large
number of presumably rich persons, and did their
best to put you at your ease by protesting, rather
too much, that the whole business was a formality, and that their only aim was that of making
assurance doubly sure. Bredon was called early
in the list, simply because he had been one of the
first to examine the body after its discovery. He
had no difficulty in identifying the deceased
gentleman, though he had not known him for
long, indeed, only for some thirty-six hours. He
would not describe himself as having been on
intimate terms with him. (Strange how, the
moment you touched officialism, you found
yourself dealing with stereotyped formulæ which
turned everything into black and white.)

" Let's see, Mr. Bredon, you were called up
early this morning – about what time would that
be ? "

" Just on a quarter past six. I looked at my
watch to see."

" And you went out at once with Mr. Halliford ? "

" Yes, after I'd put a few clothes on. Naturally I didn't wait for anything else."

" And you went straight to the silo ? "

" Yes, down the drive."

" You went in alone and examined the body ? "

" Yes."

" And you were satisfied at once that life was extinct ? You didn't suggest moving the body outside and trying to restore respiration ? Now, Mr. Bredon, why was that ? "

" It was quite obvious the man was dead. He was black in the face, and his heart wasn't moving at all. Halliford had seen him already, and he came to the same conclusion. So I thought better leave the body until the police had seen it."

" You didn't move it at all, then ? "

" I just lifted up the head to look at the face. I saw that the collar was already undone."

" You are sure you didn't do that yourself in lifting the head ? "

" Quite impossible. I lifted it very gently."

" Did you suppose that the collar had been opened by Mr. Halliford ? "

" No, I assumed that Worsley had done it himself before he died. If Halliford had done it, he would have turned the body over, so as to get at the neck better."

" Ah, that's very likely. Was there anything

when you went in, lying in the neighbourhood of the body ; a hat, for instance ? "

" No, no hat. I found a pipe, but that was Halliford's ; he had been in the silo the afternoon before and had missed it." (It seemed best, on the whole, to mention the pipe, in case Halliford had done so ; heaven forbid that the police should start having theories about it !)

" Thank you, Mr. Bredon. Now, about last night – did it seem to you that Mr. Worsley was in his usual spirits ? "

" In good spirits, anyhow. He was very gay, I thought."

" Not feverishly gay ? Not as if he was trying to force himself to seem cheerful ? "

" Not in the least. His manner was very quiet and dry, as if he entered naturally into the spirit of the whole thing."

" And when did you last see him alive, Mr. Bredon ? "

" He left the company, I suppose, about half-past nine. I couldn't be sure within ten minutes or so."

" And where were you yourself after that ? You will excuse my asking that, but of course it is important for us to know what ground your observation covers, so that we can tell for certain where Mr. Worsley *wasn't.*"

" To be sure. I was with the rest of the company in the drawing-room, which looks out over

the river, till half-past ten. Then we went out
to the front door for a moment ; and after that
I was looking out of this window here for about
half an hour, by myself. Then, seeing Mr. and
Mrs. Halliford leaving the house——"

" You could swear to them, could you ? I
only ask because it was a dark night, of course."

" I haven't any doubt about them. There
was light coming out from a whole lot of windows
on this side, and I couldn't possibly have mistaken Worsley, say, for Halliford. Then, according to arrangement, I went out by the
french windows of the drawing-room, down the
path to the river, along the river, and up again
by the path which joins the drive near the gate.
I got straight into the car, and we drove off."

" You passed nobody on the way ? "

" I passed Mrs. Arnold just inside the drawing-
room. She was looking for a map she had left
there. I saw nobody else close to, though Miss
Morel got into her car and drove off just ahead
of us – I knew who it was because of the car."

" Now, Mr. Bredon, just in case it should be
necessary, I should like to know how much the
other members of the party were under your
observation all this time."

" They were all there in the drawing-room,
except Worsley and from about twenty past ten
onwards Mr. Halliford – he had gone down to
open the drive gates. All the rest of us were

there in the front hall at half-past ten, but Mrs. Halliford just drove up beyond the gate for two or three minutes, shouting to her husband to come in ; she left the car in front of the others in the drive and came straight back to us. About five minutes later I could make out, from the shadows on the drive, that the whole party were there at their stations ; that didn't, of course, include Worsley."

" It's not a very easy job swearing to shadows, Mr. Bredon. Did you keep them under observation the whole time ? "

" Of course not. I could be certain of Mrs. Halliford, whose window was just above mine, and of Mr. Carberry, whose window was just opposite mine. I should have noticed if either of them had been away from the window for, say, five minutes. When the race had started, we were driving by ourselves, so that I can only answer for my wife and myself – and for Miss Morel, but I think you have some record of her movements, haven't you ? We reached the garage at King's Norton at 12.58 and found the Hallifords already there ; the Arnolds drove up about a quarter of an hour later, and the Carberrys a few minutes after them."

" And you can't give any guess, yourself, when it was that the unfortunate gentleman met his end ? "

" I suppose it will have been soon after we left.

Assuming, that is, that he committed suicide. He would have waited, surely, till he knew that the coast was clear."

"Well, that's only an opinion. He might have left by the front, while you were all in the drawing-room, or by the river path while you were all in the front of the house."

(Now, did one tell the police about those finds in the walled garden ? On the whole, not ; it was up to them to look round if they wanted to.) "He might, of course. But he couldn't tell, if he left before half-past ten, that we shouldn't miss him ; and after half-past ten he was liable at any moment to find the river path a mass of stampeding humanity. All I can say is that in his place I should have waited till the race started."

"Thank you. Now, I think you said Mr. Halliford left the house at about twenty minutes past ten to open the drive gate, and that Mrs. Halliford was calling out for him some few minutes after half past. Have you any idea why she did not meet him coming back from the gate or what he was doing all that time ? You cannot answer to having seen his shadow, even, till about 10.40, or himself till eleven o'clock. Please don't understand me as suggesting anything unpleasant, but it's important to get everybody's movements fixed, and then we know where we are. You did not

89

see anything of Mr. Halliford during that interval ? ''

" No ; I suppose the best way would be to ask him himself. What I imagined at the time was that he had gone down the path from the drive gate to the river, and was walking back that way. Of course, he might have made a cut through the walled garden ; but in that case I should have expected to see him coming in."

" Would it be natural for him to go round by the river path ? It's longer, surely ? ''

" Yes, one wouldn't choose it if one was in a hurry. But he wasn't in a hurry, and the river bank makes a nice stroll. He may have wanted to shut the wicket gate at the bottom of the slope, so that we should take longer getting round to our cars."

" That's certainly possible. On the other hand, you can say that you had Mrs. Halliford under observation all the time from nine o'clock till eleven, when she drove off for King's Norton ? ''

" Not actually under observation ; she was within earshot, but not in sight, when she drove the car out and called for her husband. We heard her shouting ; but at that distance, and in the dark, we couldn't see her."

" And how long did she take over that, about ? ''

" Less than ten minutes, certainly ; I should say not much above five."

" Thank you ! Now, will you try to remember whether you saw any human being in the neighbourhood of the silo when you and Mrs. Bredon drove out on your way to King's Norton ? I don't mean of your own party, they are accounted for ; but there are a good many servants in the house, and any of them might have been out. You are certain you saw no one ? "

" Positive. And, mark you, I think I should have noticed if there had been anybody there. You see, the servants were warned not to be about in the drive then, because we wanted to have a flying start for the race, without fear of accidents."

" H'm ; just so." (It was evident that the Hereford police were no fonder of eloping races than Bredon himself.) " And now, just one more thing," added the inspector, turning round in his chair but not altering his voice at all, " – would it surprise you to hear that somebody thought they saw you in the drive at a quarter to eleven ? "

" Not in the least. It wouldn't surprise me, because I've got a friend at Scotland Yard, and I've often discussed police methods of interrogation with him. We don't quite see eye to eye about some of them."

91

" Well, well," said the inspector, " you have me there. You must excuse us, Mr. Bredon, we try to do our best. And, between ourselves, this Mr. Worsley was a well-known man, and there are people up in London who are bothering us about this business a good deal. I'm very grateful to you for all you've told me. Would it be fair, now, to ask the name of your friend at Scotland Yard ? "

" Certainly ; man called Leyland, who was in the same regiment with me all the last part of the War. He'll give me quite a good character."

And Bredon was dismissed, marvelling once more at the great unimaginative thoroughness of those who guard the public peace.

CHAPTER X: THE GARDEN AFTER
BREAKFAST

THE POLICE HAD a long morning of it. Most
of the house-party seemed to be put through
much the same catechism as Bredon's, and came
out of it apparently unruffled – all except Phyllis
Morel, who found her style hopelessly cramped
(she explained) because the functionary who
accompanied the inspector nudged his elbow
and whispered something when she came in.
She knew at once that she had been recognised
as last night's transgressor of the speed limit :
" My dear, they looked handcuffs at me all the
time. I felt like a sort of rake's progress – show
me the woman who drives through Hereford at
fifty close on midnight, and I will show you
the woman who pitched a total stranger down
the silo an hour earlier ; that sort of thing.
It's no use having an honest face when there's
a previous conviction against you ; they didn't
believe a word I said." Tollard, by his own
account, seemed to have had the most severe
examination. His car had been held up by a
mysterious stoppage only about a mile from

the house ; the Carberrys had passed him at full speed, and it was only the luck of a passing lorry that enabled him to take the road again. By that time, it was too late to take part in the race, and he had returned to Lastbury at a quarter past twelve ; no servants were to be seen, and, since the rest of the house-party were absent, nobody could swear to his movements.

Meanwhile, the servants remained to be interviewed. In that carelessly organised household the staff was usually engaged on a short-term system with a minimum of references; their comings and goings were subject to little control, and less so than usual on a night when they believed the whole party to have left the house for a joyride. It was while this interminable process dragged on that Mrs. Halliford suddenly descended on Miles Bredon and carried him off for a private talk in the walled garden. " We shall be undisturbed there," she said, " and I am so anxious to have just a word or two." Bredon was appalled by the prospect ; he disliked Mrs. Halliford at the best of times, and Mrs. Halliford in the rôle of unstrung female promised to be an absolute nightmare. But there was no help for it, and Angela's declaration that she was going up on to the roof with a pair of field-glasses seemed ill timed.

" I suppose you think Cecil committed

suicide ? " Mrs. Halliford began. She was being " brave," you felt ; she had the air of one opening her heart with reluctance, not asking for sympathy but too proud to conceal how much she cared.

No pair of walkers are worse matched than one who has eyes for outside things and one whose attention is monopolised by concentration within. Go for a walk along country lanes in spring with a man who is discussing his private difficulties or ambitions, and you will be disgusted to find how the peeping of buds and the stirring of new life in the hedgerows passes him by unnoticed – or vice versa, for introversion and extroversion come to us by turns. On this occasion, there was no reason on the surface of things why Bredon's mind should have been directed outwards. Nothing can be more lovely than a walled garden in summer, but the one at Lastbury grew haphazard, at the whim of a gardener who found vegetables more profitable to him personally than flowers. The sweet peas were only a kind of mask to prevent awkward inquiries into asparagus statistics ; pinks and pansies were only decoys to distract the eye from the state of the raspberry canes. But Bredon, as soon as the gate had closed behind them, had become aware of something which interested him much more than either flowers or vegetables. The paper crown, which he had last seen lying close to the side of the central path, was there no longer. He was raking the bushes in search of it, puzzling his brains over its disappearance, as he kept up, with mechanical politeness, his side of the conversation.

" I don't think I've any clear idea," he said. " It's hardly my business to make guesses, is it ? I suppose really we all know so little of each other's troubles that we are prepared to suspect suicide anywhere. How is one to know that one's best friend doesn't, secretly, find life an intolerable burden ? " That was the right note ; she would want one to say that sort of thing. Meanwhile, where on earth had that paper cap disappeared to ? Why hadn't he annexed it at the time, instead of leaving it for some officious gardener to tidy away ?

" I think you're wrong there," said his hostess. " At least, I dare say you are right about not knowing other people's troubles ; though I think I knew Cecil through and through. But in most suicides there's an element of selfishness, and I don't believe Cecil was capable of that kind of selfishness. So many other people's lives depended on him, and he knew it. He lived very much for his friends, and I don't believe that he'd have taken the unfair way out, however much he had been depressed by public worries ; he thought of his friends first. Of course, I know what you'll say ; you'll say it's impossible anybody should have wanted to be clambering about in a silo at dead of night. But, you know, I shouldn't be in the least surprised if that, too, was part of his wonderful unselfishness. You heard Walter saying yesterday afternoon that he had lost his pipe and wondering whether he could have left it in the silo. Well, it *was* in the silo, and I can't help wondering whether Cecil didn't go out to look for it and find it just before those dreadful fumes overcame him. That was just the sort of man he was ; he would waste time doing the most insignificant things for his friends. But I suppose that strikes you as far-fetched ? "

" Oh, I think it's perfectly possible." Yes, there was no doubt they had passed, by now, the place where the cap had been ; and now nobody except Bredon himself could bear witness that it had ever lain there. Confound these tidy people ! At this rate, the cigar-end might have been cleared away too. " Of course, he didn't carry an electric torch ; at least, there was none found on the body. But he may have struck matches, and it would be easy for them to slip in between the stalks, so that they wouldn't be found. As a matter of fact, I was saying to my wife just now that it

97

didn't look to me like suicide. The action of the gas in such cases is so uncertain. One wonders if Worsley would even know that the gas was poisonous."

" Well, as a matter of fact he did. I remember talking to him about the silo when it was first put up. He knew a good deal about agriculture, in his omniscient way, and I remember his cautioning me about the gas. Now, look here, Mr. Bredon, I want to ask a favour of you. I know you're a very busy man, and I'm sure Mrs. Bredon is a home-loving person who doesn't like long visits. And I'm afraid this will be a sad place for all of us after what's happened. But I do wish you could see your way to staying on here for a few days, even after the inquest. It's not for my sake so much ; it's for Walter's."

" It's very good of you indeed ; I shall be delighted to stay on if I may." Well, of all the abominable luck ! Here they were at the end of the path, and no cigar-end ! If he had known there was going to be an annual conference of the Anti-Litter League meeting that morning, he would have done their work for them before breakfast. Well, the only thing was to keep his eyes open, on the off chance that other traces might be left, less conspicuous to the eye. " The only thing is, of course I have to be at the disposal of the Company, and they might send for me at any moment. But . . . do you mean there's any special way in which I can help Mr. Halliford ? "

" No special way, no ; but I do want him to have a friend about. It's horrid to have to say it, but he doesn't really care for any of these other people at all. I asked them because I thought it would amuse him, but he says they get on his nerves. He likes you, Mr. Bredon, and I believe you can do him good. He has been terribly run down, what with business anxieties and one thing and another ; and of course when one's like that one's instinct is always to mope about alone, but it isn't good for one, is it ? And then, I'm so afraid this terrible shock – Cecil was a great, great friend of his – will make him still worse ; I'm really afraid of melancholia. So if you could stay on here and try to take him out of himself a bit, just be interested in the farm and get him to take you out on the river and all that sort of thing, it would be a true kindness. There ! I'm afraid you think I'm presuming on a very short acquaintance, Mr. Bredon."

" Oh, but I shall really be delighted ; you mustn't talk of it as a favour." The hundredth chance again ! There was, after all, one piece of evidence he had overlooked ; probably it had been lying under the paper cap when he first passed. It was a white favour, of the kind they had all worn at dinner yesterday evening. And that, of course, was as good as the cap any day ; it proved that a member of the party had gone down the garden path after dinner. No, it was better than the cap ; it almost proved that it was Worsley who had gone down the garden path. For the white favour was supposed to be a badge they would all wear during the race ; who, then, would be likely to throw his away ? Only the man who knew that he was not chosen to be one of the hares, and could not, since he did not drive, be one of the hounds. No favour had been found on the body. This was excellent ; but how to make sure that some officious brute did not tidy this away too ? Or would it be best to draw his hostess's attention to it ? He would, if they passed that way again. " This is such a lovely part of the world ; I was hating the idea of having to go off again at once."

They reached the gate at the house end of the garden, and still Mrs. Halliford went on pouring out her gratitude and her anxieties, still kept her guest by her side as she turned round and walked up the path again. There was a fortunate pause in her talk as they came to the middle of the path, and Bredon seized on the opportunity. " Mrs. Halliford," he said, " I'm only a guest in the house, and the police have had their money's worth out of me ; I'm not

going out of my way to help them. But I want
to call your attention to something which might
help them, if you think it's wise – I leave that
to you. I'm sorry to inflict this on you, because
I know it will revive painful memories, but . . .
look here ! '' and he pointed to the telltale bow
of white ribbon which lay beside them on the
edge of the flower-border.

Mrs. Halliford peered down at it as if dazed ;
then suddenly straightened herself. " I know
what you mean," she said ; " it was his bow,
obviously. And the police may think that he
threw it aside with a despairing gesture as he
went down this path to take his own life. Well,
if they think that, I can't help it. I feel sure
one ought to help them all one can. But it's
good of you, it's like you, to be so considerate.
I think – I think I'll go and tell them now."
And she left Bredon at the gate, still showering
compliments. He did not waste time ; one
thing he must do before the police came on the
scene and began to regard his intrusion as
officious – he must make sure of his facts about
that thermometer at the further end. He
retraced his way down the path with a few quick
strides, took one more vain look for the vanished
cigar-end, and then devoted his attention to the
thermometer. The temperature had risen, as
the sun had gained in strength and the mist
had dispersed ; it stood, now, at 70. The

minimum index still registered 59 as the lowest temperature during the night. But the maximum index, which had stood, an hour or two ago, at 68 with the mercury, was now standing at 72. A circumstance which perhaps excused his ejaculation, " Well, I'm damned ! "

" No, IT'S NOT the least little bit of use," Bredon said to himself. " It doesn't begin to make sense – yet. Somebody went through the walled garden last night, or late yesterday afternoon, anyhow, and played with that maximum-and-minimum thermometer ; pulled back both indices to meet the mercury and left it. In the night the temperature cooled to 59, and the minimum index was pushed to 59 and left sticking there ; all that's in good order. At about eight in the morning the temperature had gone up to 68, carrying the maximum index with it. By noon or thereabouts the mercury had gone up to 70 and the maximum index to 72. Which is impossible. Therefore somebody, between eight this morning and noon, thought it worth while to pretend that the thermometer hadn't been played with last night after all. If that somebody was the same as the somebody mentioned above, it wasn't Worsley ; dead men don't play with thermometers. And it begins to look as if it might be this somebody, and not an over tidy gardener, who took away that cap

103

and that cigar-end. Overlooking, apparently, the white bow, which was under or near the cap. That is to say, somebody is engaged, has been engaged this morning since eight, in covering somebody's tracks. But what the devil would be the use of going to that policeman and telling him about it ? If only one had a real policeman, a man like Leyland, to deal with, it would be worth putting him wise. But these Hereford people would be hopeless ; probably they'd want to know whether the paper cap was size 7 or size 8. Lord, if I had any status here I'd have some fun with it all."

The day was one of exquisite discomfort. The Arnolds, who lived near and were known locally, motored off home ; the rest of the party were requested, politely but unmistakably, to stay on till the inquest. It seemed heartless, at such a time, to leave the house with any obvious intention of enjoying yourself ; yet in the house, or even in the grounds, you were plainly an encumbrance. The police, tired out but imperturbably thorough, were measuring the innumerable car-tracks left in the dust by last night's adventure ; reporters were being turned away briskly from the front door ; in the billiard-room the doctor was conducting an autopsy ; the telephone bell was ringing all the time, with messages of inquiry from relations of the dead man, messages of sympathy from friends. The abominable monkey walked with tail erect from room to room, registering a kind of human interest without any trace of human emotion, or sat in the middle of the drive, parodying with an imaginary tape-measure the undignified movements of the police. Walter Halliford, pale but wonderfully calm, dealt with all the nightmare business of the situation single-handed ; nobody could help him, nobody liked to look as if they were avoiding his company. The sun blazed down pitilessly, as if mocking by its impartial good humour the private griefs of a single household ; and through the hot air throbbed, ceaselessly, the roar of the silo engine, free to ply its task now that the crop had been eased of its funereal burden. Men might come and men might go, but still the giant had to be fed, hand over hand, storing up endlessly in its grim vault the chopped stalks that were food for beast and poison for man.

The Bredons found the atmosphere of discomfort intolerable and soon after luncheon went off together in a canoe, to bathe higher up the river. For the shock of communicated sorrow, and for fruitless cudgelling of the brains, there is no remedy like air and exercise ; and if the day afforded little of the one, the Wye promised plenty of the other. The Wye is not a ladies' river ; once you have turned the head of your boat upstream you must work, and work feverishly, in its frequent rapids. They were drifting back easily late in the afternoon when they were suddenly hailed by a shout from a bank which had seemed altogether deserted ; and marked, with some surprise, a camper in shorts and very little else beckoning to them from the further bank. It was with considerable effort that they stayed their course and began heading up and across the stream ; the management of the boat left them little opportunity for looking round, and it was not till they were close in that Miles gave tongue in recognition. " Leyland ! " he cried, " what on earth are you doing here ? " And, as they drew in to shore, " Is this a police decoy ? Investigating hiker scandals or something of that kind ? How did you know it was us ? "

Leyland held the boat for them to get out and fastened it. " I knew it was you," he said, " because I was looking for you. Discreet inquiries showed that you had gone up river. I say, I'm here incognitissimo, and don't you forget it. That hedge there, as I dare say you don't know, is the exact limit of the Lastbury estate. And, as I'm not in a position to call at Lastbury, I thought I would pitch my tent as near the edge as possible. Gad, this is luck ; I hadn't the least idea how I was going to make contact with you."

" Oo, I say," murmured Angela, looking

round her, " can you really do this sort of thing ?
The whole boy scout business, I mean, rubbing
two sticks together and roasting an eel over
them ? But what luck that you should happen
to be here ! "

" I don't happen, Mrs. Bredon ; I go where
I'm sent. And I'm sent here, if you'll believe
me, because you're here."

" There you are, Miles dear ; I knew they'd
get on your track sooner or later."

" No, it's not quite that this time. The point
is, people up above have found out, God knows
how, that you're here and that you're friends
of mine. So, as they can't give me any official
position here, I've got to use you as a stalking-
horse ; that is, if you'll let me."

" But, good Lord, Leyland," objected Bredon,
" why are you here at all if you haven't got any
official position ? Has the Yard been called in
or hasn't it ? The local sleuths are still pretty
busy."

" Don't you make any mistake about that ;
the Yard isn't on in this thing, and I don't
suppose it's going to be. The local police will
have the management of it, and at the inquest
it will be just another of these suicides. But –
well, perhaps I oughtn't to say any more.
Here I am, that's all."

" Let us in a bit more than that," pleaded
Angela. " We're terribly discreet, you know."

" Well, as a matter of fact I know very little, and there's very little of that that I'm supposed to know. But roughly it's this – people on top have begun to get worried about all these suicides of important people, bankers and what not, and somebody seems to have got the idea that they may not be all they seem."

"What, you mean a sort of assassination business ? " asked Miles.

" That sort of thing. Personally, I don't mind telling you I think they're barking up the wrong tree. They want to make out, for instance, that the thing is worked from abroad ; and, you see, there aren't any foreigners on in this act."

" Miles, he's beginning to pump us. He thinks we shall tell him about Phyllis Morel. Sorry, Mr. Leyland, but she really isn't French in the least ; I mean, not in the sense of having any sort of home in France or relations over there she ever writes to. At least, so I'm told."

" No, really, I wasn't fishing. I've come to put myself in your hands absolutely ; you must tell me as much or as little as you like. Only – well, if there is any dirty work going on, I was hoping you'd help the ends of justice, and, some think, of civilisation, by giving me the hang of it."

" That's all very fine," said Bredon, " but where do I come in exactly ? Oh, I know, I've lost all claim to be considered a gentleman ever since I took on work as a spy. But, curse it all, it's one thing to form one's own impressions of the house-party one's staying with, it's another to dish out information to the police which may for all one knows land one's host and hostess——"

"Oh, you can count them out all right," explained Leyland. "They're not on the map at all; nobody could have wanted Worsley dead less than they did. What, didn't you know? Well, I suppose it is rather confidential. Halliford's on the rocks; his business has been going down for years past, and there's only one thing that could set him on his feet again, which is a particular commercial agreement – well, I won't specify. Anyhow, the point is that Worsley was running this agreement for all he was worth; shouldn't wonder if he did it to help them, partly. And now he's dead, it very likely won't come off at all. No, if there were two people in the world whose interests was to keep Worsley jolly well wrapped up in cotton wool, it was the Hallifords."

"I didn't know that," admitted Bredon. "Still, there are these other people living in the same house with me . . . I'll tell you what I'll do. You shall know all I know already, because that is knowledge which has simply come to me; I haven't spied and questioned to get it. But anything I find out from now on, I may tell you or I may not; I must decide as I feel about

it. I don't mind telling you, Leyland, that I'm
rather glad to have you about here. It's not
an atmosphere I feel comfortable in, somehow.
It's . . . what *is* there about it, Angela ? "

" I think I know what you mean, and I think
I know why you feel like that. It's because,
surely, the Hallifords aren't entertaining their
friends : they are just a job lot of people. Or
rather, *we* are a job lot of people. If you come
to think of it, we are the jobbest of the lot."

" Well," said Leyland, " I shall be here till
the inquest's over, and probably longer. You've
only to whistle for me any time you want me.
As well as I can see, that path which goes along
the river comes right up to the hedge here, and
I'm only ten minutes' walk or so from the house.
But I don't think it would be a very good thing
for you to be seen talking to me, so perhaps it
would be best if you stroll right across this field
and into the wood opposite. Then, if I'm in
sight – and I shall be most of the time – I'll
come and join you. We'd better have an
assignation for to-morrow, though ; shall we
say noon ? By that time, I ought to have got
the police reports forwarded to me ; one can
arrange for that on a job of this kind. And you
can tell me just what you think fit ; I won't
press you."

" All right," said Bredon. " But I'll tell you
one thing straight away : this Halliford man,

by his wife's account of him, is all on edge ; he was having bad nerves before all this show started. Well, it's probably jolted him up a good deal, and she's afraid of what may happen. So, if you're hanging about here by the river bank, you might keep a look out and see that he doesn't drop in on the quiet. I know you policemen don't really care a hang about life-saving ; but we don't want more suicides about than we can help."

" Besides," added Angela, " you forget that Mr. Leyland is a boy scout now ; it will be all in his line of business. Well, good night, Mr. Leyland, and good luck with the horse-flies. I'd sooner it was you than me."

CHAPTER XII : THE EMPTY HOUSE

THE NEXT MORNING the weather still held, but the mist was thicker and there was less promise of its disappearance. The inquest was to be in the afternoon, and Bredon was relieved by the prospect of talking over his discoveries with a representative of the police before he decided whether he ought to say anything about them to the coroner or not. He found Leyland already sitting on the stile that led into the wood, with a formidable set of depositions in his hand.

" I never knew a case where people were so remarkable by their absence," he explained. " They had to put those servants through the deuce of a lot of questioning before they could find out what was up ; and do you know what they did ? Why, at half-past eleven the whole crowd of them went off in the motor-boat, with gramophone complete. All except the butler ; he sleeps at the lodge. Shows that servants have a pretty good idea what their employers' plans are."

Bredon knitted his brows. " You bet it does ; but there's one thing you don't seem to have realised which puts the lid on it. Had they the brass to do that, or even to arrange it, when they weren't certain whether Worsley was in the house or not? You see, he wasn't due to take part in the race unless he was chosen as an eloping partner. Did they assume he was in bed, or what?"

"They don't seem to have asked about that. Probably assumed that Mrs. Halliford had picked him up as her partner; they were pretty thick, you know. Anyhow, it means that if the death happened between half-past eleven and half-past twelve, it can't be murder very well; there doesn't seem to have been a soul on the spot."

"Why half-past twelve?"

"That's when Miss Morel came back; says she did, anyhow. She can't have been very much earlier, because of course the police had her timed at Hereford."

"It would be a dashed smart idea," said Bredon, chuckling, "to establish an alibi by getting yourself into trouble with a policeman on point duty. Still, you've nothing against her, have you?"

"Nothing against anybody. Except perhaps this Tollard fellow. His times seem to be all wrong. He must have started with the rest of you, because these Carberrys passed him on the road, so he was ahead of them. Then he says he had engine trouble about a mile from the gate. Is that very likely? I mean, wouldn't one be rather careful about that before starting on a race?"

"Angela was certainly. And I heard Tollard say he was going to overhaul his car. Must have forgotten about it."

"Well then he says he thought it wasn't worth while to walk back to the house because somebody was certain to pass before long; he was nearly on the main road, you see, by then. He says he got back about a quarter past twelve, before Miss Morel. She says she passed him on the road, later than that, about twenty-five past."

"Why didn't she stop? Didn't he signal?"

"Yes, but she never does stop, she says; too many car bandits about. God knows that's reasonable. But she recognised afterwards that it must have been Tollard, partly because the place where he was left corresponded exactly, partly because she heard him drive up, she says, a quarter of an hour or so after she got in, 12.45 or a little later."

"You think Tollard is lying?"

"Looks as if he might be. But it doesn't work out very well. I mean, if he was mixed up in this business at all, presumably he left his car where it was, walked to Lastbury, and then walked back to his car again. Which is

perfectly consistent with the time he gives –
12.15 – for bringing his car back. Why didn't
he make it a quarter *to* twelve, which would
have left no time for the walk ? Or a quarter to
one, which would mean, at any rate, that he
would have one witness to his movements ? "

" Yes, but if he'd said a quarter to twelve,
that might have been before Worsley's death.
And if he'd said a quarter to one – upon my
word, I don't know why he didn't say a quarter
to one. Looks to me as if Phyllis Morel was
lying when she said she passed him, but what
on earth for ? "

" Anyhow, neither of them has a strict alibi.
The death might have been as late as one – just ;
so the doctor says. But I don't see how they
are going to be connected with the thing ; confound it all, where's the motive ? "

" Nobody had a motive that I can see, if it
comes to that. Tollard talks revolution, of
course, like most of these young men nowadays,
but I don't see him as a thug."

" You mean you like him ? "

" No, but he's not my idea of a thug. Oh
yes, I see you know all about that old story,
but that's different. Anyhow, I don't see
Tollard as a silo-thug, if I may coin the expression. It takes strength to hoist a man into a
silo, even if he's a light-weight, even if he's dead.
To do it while he's still alive needs even more in

the way of stamina – unless you lure him in under false pretences, of course. What could one do ? Ask him to come and join in a rat hunt ? "

" He may have suffocated him in his bed."

" And then parked him in the silo ? I don't see him doing it ; he's a little man, and it would be the devil of a weight, even if he used the pulley. That pulley doesn't work any too easily ; I've tried it."

" Well, I'm going to keep an eye on him, any-how. Meanwhile, you were going to tell me one or two things, weren't you ? "

Bredon sketched in, as well as he could, the missing details of the story : his impressions of the people, Mrs. Halliford's chronicle of their past careers, the exact stages by which the deter-mination to try the eloping race had been evolved, finally, the story of what he had found, and of what he had failed to find in the walled garden. At the mention of these last experiences Leyland's eye brightened and he slapped his thigh with sudden animation.

" But that's tremendously important – about the thermometer, I mean. I don't think you've seen the bearing of it, because you've tried to connect the alteration of the thermometer with the disappearance of the cigar-end and the paper cap. But anybody might tidy up things like that ; probably a gardener goes round every morning and clears away the things that are left on the main path in case the family should be taking a stroll after breakfast. Isolate this business of the thermometer, and the bearing of it is surely obvious. Nobody knew that you had seen it ; somebody, after breakfast presumably, deliberately faked the reading. It did, as a matter of fact, turn rather cold that night, colder than most of the days we'd been having. It was, it appears, in somebody's interest to pretend that the night had been less cold than in fact it was. What would be the use of that, to a person concerned in a murder? There's only one possible answer : unexpected cold may hasten on coldness in the body of the victim so as to make it appear that he has been dead longer than he actually has. The somebody, then, was somebody who had committed a murder, or been party to the committing of a murder, rather early that night, but wanted it to appear that the death had happened rather late that night."

" You know, that's extraordinarily ingenious. The only bother is, you've got the facts wrong. Your criminal wanted, for his purposes, to play billy with the minimum index. He didn't, he played billy with the maximum. He didn't artificially conceal the cold of the night before, he artificially revealed the heat of the day before – 72 in the shade."

" Ye-es, that's true. But . . . look here, I'll

117

tell you what he did ; he *exaggerated* the heat of the day before, and on purpose. Why ? Because a heat as big as that – it was only about 70, really – would neutralise the usual cold of the silo, after banking up all day like that. And therefore a corpse would be rather slow about going cold in such a temperature. So, if he could make us think the silo was very hot that evening, he might persuade us to believe that a body which had really been dead only since half-past one had been dead since half-past eleven."

" It was rather a big assumption that the doctor would consult a thermometer, and that thermometer."

" So he would have, if he'd known his business. These country G.P.'s do everything by rule of thumb."

" That's always the way with you, Leyland ; you get it into your head that somebody is at the heart of the mystery, and every bit of evidence that crops up is always made to fit in. Confess now, it's the handcuffs for Tollard ? "

" Oh, I keep an open mind. But I don't see why you're so certain he's all right, except that he's not much of a strong man."

" Well, I believe the real reason why I don't take Tollard into account is because he so obviously didn't want the eloping party. If he had any game on, it was so clearly in his interest that the race should happen. But, so far as he was concerned, he did his best to call the thing off."

" And that's your fixed idea, you know. You won't allow for the eloping race being a mere accident ; you think it must have been part of a deliberate plan leading up to murder. Why shouldn't it be just the other way round – that there was a deliberate plan leading up to murder, and the eloping race came in as an unwelcome accident, which actually modified the course of events and perhaps complicated them ? Suppose that the idea of the race had never turned up – where did Tollard sleep ? "

" In the bachelors' quarters, they're called ; at the west end of the house."

" And Worsley ? "

" He slept there too, naturally."

" There you are. All Tollard had got to do was to go in and spifflicate him in the bed-clothes, and you married people none the wiser. What did he want with any eloping race ? But, if there was to be an eloping race, and Worsley was going to be left behind, the best thing was for Tollard to have an imaginary breakdown and finish off his job while there was nobody in the house. Mind, I don't say that's what happened. I only say that, if I've got to suspect people, I prefer to start by suspecting the people who can't account for their movements."

" I've no doubt the coroner's jury will do the same."

" Don't you believe it. There isn't going to be any trouble for anybody at the inquest. You see, if there's anything at all fishy about this business, it's not got to be made public. This isn't law and order ; it's politics."

CHAPTER XIII : HOW GAS IS GENERATED

LEYLAND'S FORECAST OF the inquest was abundantly justified. The coroner knew what was expected of him, and impatiently brushed aside any suggestion that foul play, or even suicide, might be the cause of Worsley's death. The servants were so carefully interrogated that no word of their midnight expedition on the river was mentioned ; the public was left to imagine that they had all been in their beds by half-past eleven. Tollard was induced to say that he got home at 12.15 "or it might have been a bit later " ; Phyllis Morel could not positively swear that she was not back by 12.25, had to admit that the car she passed on the road might have been another car and that she might have mistaken some irrelevant noise on the main road for that of Tollard's return. The theory – put forward by Halliford himself – that Worsley might have gone into the silo to retrieve the lost pipe was treated as if it were self-evidently true, and the question how he proposed to find the object without either matches or torch was conveniently shelved.

121

The eloping race, which might otherwise have made good copy for the sensational Press, was disguised as a " midnight expedition to King's Norton," as if that town were the Mecca of the sleepless. It was perhaps noticeable that Bredon, when called, was not asked to give any account of his profession.

As if with the idea of centring interest elsewhere, the coroner spread himself on the question of silos, their construction, their ventilation, their dangers, their utility. An expert witness was called from the nearest available university to tell the jury – who were mostly farmers already – all he knew about it. Those patient newspaper-readers who are always ready to follow up a mystery, to form their own theories about it, and to communicate these (with no thought of remuneration) to the police, found themselves put off by an interminable discussion of agricultural technicalities. How dry ought the crop to be exactly ? How closely ought it to be pressed down ? What would be the extent and nature of the fermentation in a given set of circumstances ? Would the witness describe those circumstances as normal circumstances ? Had it been determined whether any gases other than carbon dioxide were likely to be generated ? If so, were those gases of an inflammable character ? and so on endlessly. Nor did the coroner, in his closing allocution, fail to recommend that all silos should be ventilated to the extreme limit which would not affect their efficiency ; that no labourer should enter a silo in the morning until it had been ascertained that no dangerous gases had been generated by the crop stacked overnight ; that no door should be sealed unless it was absolutely certain that the silage could not possibly sink below the level of that door ; in a word, he gave it to be understood that silos were very tricky things to deal with, and one newspaper of the cheaper type hardly exaggerated the situation when it printed THE SILO MENACE as its chief headline. But the more human question, why a public man should want to spend the later part of the evening in such an edifice, was never answered because it was never asked.

As to the identity of the deceased gentleman, the newspaper editors were not less discreet. The *Times* obituary, from its length and its prominence, gave you clearly to understand that a great figure had passed out of that world in which the editors of newspapers move but their readers do not. Yet, when you came to look into it, it was difficult to discover what Cecil Worsley had done, or even been, that all this encomium should be lavished on him. You learned that he had a rare gift of personal friendship and that his collection of old china was probably unique. The writers of the gossip columns had much to say about the eccentricities of his great-aunt, so well known in the salons of the nineties, and about the remarkable Sealyhams bred by one of his first cousins in Dorsetshire. Sympathy was expressed everywhere, even in the *Reaper and Binder*, which, however, insinuated that it was impossible to make a silo absolutely foolproof.

There was one lamentable exception to this conspiracy of correct behaviour. One paper there was which, for no more reason than it had for most of its occasional stunts, took this opportunity to make an outcry against aliens, anarchists and undesirables generally. The article, which sprawled over its most important page, was written with all that finesse in which modern journalists are adept. That is to say, it was plain to the meanest intelligence that it referred to the " Lastbury Mystery," which jostled it for space in an adjoining column. But there was nothing to say so ; nothing to convict the paper, therefore, of a notorious attempt to prejudge the coroner's findings. It trotted out five or six other cases in which men of importance in the financial or political world had been found shot, drowned, etc., and asked whether the arm of coincidence was really long enough to account for all this ? Suggestions had been made in certain quarters (a convenient phrase) that it was all part of a concerted plot to wreck the harmony of Europe at a moment of acute trial. People were beginning to ask themselves (another useful one) whether our public men were sufficiently protected from the results of that odium which they incurred by their patriotic activities. A distinguished police official in an unnamed European country had talked mysteriously about a Black Hand which was organising a veritable campaign of secret assassination. Documents had come to light not long since in a certain European capital which, if and when they were published, would create a considerable stir by their frank disclosure of the forces at work to disorganise the world's markets. A cartoon from a Russian paper was here reproduced, representing a capitalist hanging from a lamp-post. And much more in the same strain ; never a fact that could be verified ; never a positive assertion that could be challenged ; above all, no reference to Lastbury. You knew that this particular stunt would have to run its course like an infantile disease, " starred " in the next two or three issues, then relegated to back pages and correspondence columns, then disappearing as suddenly as it had arisen, with nothing done and nothing even attempted as the result of it. The " rumour " that a question was to be asked in Parliament you knew at once to be false. The question what the police were doing to justify their existence was its appropriate and inevitable finale.

Bredon found Leyland gloomily assimilating this document as he came away from the inquest. They stood for a little leaning over the bridge, where Leyland was pretending to exercise the fishing rights he had been careful to acquire from a local syndicate. " It's all very well for you to laugh at that kind of thing," he said, " and of course I know as well as you that it's just blah. Some fool has been over-hearing things he oughtn't to and has been sketching out a scenario from fancy, all wrong. Why, he hadn't even got the names right. And I know that nothing will come of it ; nothing ever does. But meanwhile it puts the wind up the officials, because they're always so con-foundedly nervous about their promotions ; and that means that we get gingered up and told to produce results, even if some wretched lunatic of an East End anarchist has to suffer for it."

" Well, it's an ill wind that blows nobody good. That article will put Lastbury on the map – even the readers of a rag like that can put two and two together – and that will mean that the Indes-cribable won't touch the case at the end of a barge pole ; I mean, not in the way of challenging it. So I shall get orders to drop it, and I can stay on here as free as air and leave when I choose."

126

"You don't mean to say you want to drop the thing now, when it's all so tied up? I should have thought you'd have had more curiosity than that."

"I've always been told that the assistants in sweet-shops are allowed to eat as many sweets as they like at the start, and that in a fortnight or so they completely lose the taste for it. So it's been with me since I took up spy work. It's killed the very instinct of curiosity in me, so that I can pass by a crowd gathered in the street without so much as looking round to see what's happening. When I'm right on to a case like this, I admit that for the first twenty-four hours or so I'm as keen as mustard. After that, if the thing is still a problem, I take no more notice of it than of yesterday's crossword. The coroner thinks it's an accident, and who am I that I should set up my judgment against his? What a man! What an agriculturalist!"

"Rot; you don't believe all that stuff. I've got some notes here about the results of the police search which make the whole case much queerer than ever. Stick them in your pocket and read them later. Look out! Here's somebody coming."

Bredon, as he pocketed the bunch of papers, became aware of Tollard drifting towards them, an embarrassing visitor in such company.

"Hullo!" he said to Leyland, "you're the

chap that's camping in the wood, aren't you ?
Saw you on the bank yesterday." And, as if no
further introduction were needed, he plunged
unsuspectingly into reminiscences of the inquest.
"Good sort, that coroner," he observed.
"Didn't try to put the wind up a man like
those blasted bobbies. Never had such an easy
let down since they viva'd me for Divvers at
Oxford. *No, not Galileo, Mr. Tollard, he doesn't
come in the Acts*, they said. *Doesn't he ;* I said,
it's all one to me. And they let me through on it.
But this fellow was even better ; a little more of
that sort of thing and you'd begin to believe the
capitalist system works. Seemed to be putting
me up to what he wanted me to say all the time ;
positively wouldn't let me believe I was in by the
quarter past. Well, I thought to myself, have
it your own silly way. But I was, you know ;
I heard the bally thing strike on that stable
clock."

Bredon was in an agony of embarrassment.
All very well to insist that Tollard had only
himself to blame if he went about blurting out
confidences to strangers he hadn't even been
introduced to. But he felt, somehow, that he
was acting as sponsor for the *bona fides* of the
alleged camper. And Leyland, he knew, was
marking and weighing every word, using him
ruthlessly as a decoy. What could one say
to either of them ? He tried to turn the

conversation aside to the commonplaces of the angling world, but unsuccessfully ; Tollard kept on coming back to the subject which occupied his mind, and not for want of encouragement from the emissary of Scotland Yard.

" Suppose it's perjury really, even if the man does lead you on ; but I don't see why that should matter much. It's an extraordinary thing, if you come to think about it, that we still go on talking about perjury in a shocked voice, as if it were something one couldn't quite mention in the drawing-room ; and yet the only reason one has for disapproving of it is that people used to think one was bound to be struck dead by a thunderbolt. We ought really to have given up minding about perjury when we gave up believing in religion. But that's always the way – like Stevenson's fable of the iron ring. You feel it's stupid to go on appealing to God, so you start appealing to something called ' honour ' which is quite imaginary really. And if you ask people what they mean by honour, they start talking about gentlemen, that is, people who have more than five hundred a year. It's all pretty thin when you come to look into it."

Leyland wound in his reel meditatively. " There's just the practical convenience of it though," he urged. " They'd find it very hard to get at the truth about what happened in a case like that the other night, for instance, if all the witnesses just said anything that came into their heads."

" Oh, that's unquestionable. But then, is it really so very important to get at the truth? What is it we were all trying to find out in that stuffy room just now? Why, simply whether Worsley was a fool who didn't know that stored grasses generate carbon dioxide, or a civilised man who was too bored to go on generating carbon dioxide himself. If the jury hadn't said Death by Misadventure they'd have said Suicide while of Unsound Mind, and who really cares? It's only a choice between two kinds of accident."

" Still," persisted Leyland, " if there weren't any inquests, it would rather encourage the kind of sudden death where there isn't any accident at all."

" Foul play, you mean? Oh, of course, if there were any question of that. . . . Even so, I don't know that it's worth all the song and dance they make over it. Worsley, now I come to think of it, was a rather assassinable person ; he was always interfering with other people's business, and that's asking for trouble. I think they do these things better in the States ; I had to give evidence over there once. . . . What, you going back, Bredon? Well, I expect I'd better come too. Good afternoon, sir, and good luck.

Wonder what sort of fellow that is," he continued, as they passed out of earshot. " Schoolmaster on holiday, I should think, wouldn't you ? "

" Something of that sort, I expect," answered Bredon miserably.

THE NOTES WHICH Bredon looked through before
tea-time were not all of equal interest. Leyland
had handed on to him the painstaking results
compiled by the Herefordshire constabulary
almost verbatim ; there was much which did not
interest the detective and need not, therefore,
interest the reader. I give here only the salient
points, in the order in which Bredon set them
forth for his own edification, together with the
reflections they aroused in him.

It was clear that Worsley, although he might
have revisited the library and his article when
he left the drawing-room, had gone on to his bedroom later. The footman who valeted him
could depose to the exact changes that had
taken place between dinner-time and the time
of his death, both in his own costume and in the
room itself. First as to the pockets : *Footman
quite positive the following objects, afterwards found
on dressing-table, were in Worsley's trouser pockets
at dinner-time – silver coins totalling* 6s. 9d. *in
value, a Yale latchkey (not fitting any lock at*

Lastbury), and a silver box containing eight wax vestas. The pockets of the coat found on the body had not been emptied, apparently, and contained two pennies, a halfpenny, a book of stamps (almost empty), and a pocket comb; there was also a note-case in the breast pocket with three Treasury notes and a postal order for five shillings in it.

Already there was room for thought; considerable room for thought. If you assumed that Worsley had started going to bed and then been visited by a sudden impulse to take a stroll outside, it was odd, surely, that he should have not emptied *all* his pockets while he was about it. Conceivably it was his habit (why hadn't they asked the footman?) to empty out only the silver, as both having some value and being liable to drop unnoticed when your clothes were folded. Either that, or you must assume, surely, that the afterthought which interrupted the routine of going to bed was something sudden. Most people, Bredon reflected, would begin with the coat pockets, as being closer to the hand; but this might be an idiosyncrasy. It was a tiresome puzzle; there was no strand of conclusive argument about it, only a trivial set of oddities which just did not work out right. And then, the pocket comb! The footman had deposed that Worsley did not carry a comb " as what you might call a general thing "; nor, to be sure, had he seemed to be a man meticulously careful about his personal appearance. The problem of the comb was not so much why he had not taken it out of that side pocket as why he had ever put it in. You do not need a pocket comb for a garden ramble at midnight, or for a visit to the silo, unless you are going to have a hay-fight in it. And, talking of the silo, it was now surely clear that there was no intention of a pipe hunt when the stroll started. Bad enough that he should have attempted it without illumination ; that he should deliberately have put down a box of matches on the dressing-table before starting would surely argue an absent-mindedness more than human. No, Worsley had gone out with the intention of visiting some place where you needed a comb but not matches ; to indulge in some occupation which might make the silver drop out of your trousers but not the note-case out of your coat. That was the lesson of these perplexing details, if they had a lesson at all.

Another object found on the dressing-table was a monocle with a black silk band. The footman admits that Worsley sometimes left his monocle about by mistake, and cannot swear that it was not there at dinner-time. Fortunate that Worsley was a frequent visitor at Lastbury, so that his habits were well known. Now, how did this item fit in ? By Jove, Worsley *was* wearing his monocle at dinner ; memory supplied an unmistakable glimpse of Worsley in a paper cap and a monocle. It had either been discarded as unnecessary when he went out later on or else had been among the first things he had put aside when it was his intention to retire for the night. He was not the sort of man you would have expected to wear an eyeglass out of mere vanity, so that it was probably a genuine aid to defective sight. All the more reason why he should have taken it with him, instead of leaving it behind, if he really went out with the idea of instituting a search after the lost pipe. Once more, you were almost driven to the conclusion that the man had started going to bed and had been surprised in the first stages of the action by a new situation.

Also found on the dressing-table, a silver wrist-watch. It had not been wound up. According to the footman, it was usually left on a small table beside the bed at night-time. This was worse than ever. A watch, indeed, was one of the first things you took off, but you put it down, once for all, where you would want it for the night, and you wound it up, quite instinctively, as you did so. To leave it, unwound, on the dressing-table was either the action of a man in a great hurry or that of a man who is not going to bed yet but prefers to leave his watch in a place of safety till he does so. It was

135

time to get the data together as far as they had come in hitherto ; you must have hypotheses to work on before you began to make sense of a job like this. Either then :

(1) Worsley had already begun to retire for the night and, with that in view, had already taken off his eye-glass and emptied his trouser pockets but not yet (for some reason) his other pockets. He had just taken off his wrist-watch when some unforeseen urgency made him interrupt the action and go out into the night, arming himself with nothing except a small pocket comb.

Or (2) Worsley had not meant to retire yet but went to his bedroom to divest himself of certain encumbrances before he went out. Things which might be in danger of getting broken, like a watch or an eyeglass ; things which were liable to drop about the place, like the contents of your trouser pockets. (Not *valuables* simply ; or why leave the note-case where it was ?) At the same time, he had been careful to provide himself with a pocket comb. Well, well ! Now for the other eccentricities.

Deceased wore a denture in his upper jaw which was in his mouth when the body was found. No, on second thoughts there could be no particular significance in that, one way or the other. It was only evidence, hardly needed, that Worsley had not gone far on his way to bed before the unforeseen happened.

He had removed his braces and exchanged the golfing-shoes he was wearing for a pair of rubber-soled tennis-shoes. The golfing-shoes, studded with heavy nails, were found under the dressing-table, the braces flung over the back of a chair. The footman is quite certain that they were not in these positions when he came to tidy the room after dinner. Yes, Bredon had noticed the tennis-shoes in the silo, but had been unable to remember whether Worsley had worn these at dinner or not. This was the first faint indication yet to hand which suggested that Worsley might have gone out with the *intention* of prowling about the silo. Nailed shoes are a nuisance, rubber shoes a convenience, when you are climbing up a series of iron rings. But of course there were other motives for wearing rubber shoes – silence, for example ; and there were other things a man might want to climb besides the silo. But if there were plenty of motives for a change of shoes, what possible motive could you have for removing your braces – and hitching up your trousers, presumably, by the tightening of a band – except that you were going to indulge in some form of violent physical exercise ? You might do it for convenience in climbing, but it hardly seemed a sufficient reason. And here was the puzzling thing, if

137

you came to think of it – Worsley, whose dress
was in some ways old-fashioned, regularly wore
a starched collar ; it was such a collar that had
been found on his body, and some unexpected
strain had actually burst the front stud that
held it. If, when he went out, he anticipated
so much of bodily exertion as would make his
braces an encumbrance, why did he continue
to endure the greater embarrassment of a
starched collar ?

The same footman had produced a very
important piece of evidence which had not come
to the ears of the house-party, and (by a curious
manipulation of justice) had been suppressed
at the inquest – at Leyland's own request, it
appeared. "*Says the bell of the library rang
about ten minutes past ten that night ; that he
answered it and found Worsley sitting there
writing ; cannot be certain how he was then
dressed (e.g. shoes ?) ; that Worsley said he would
have breakfast in bed next day, about ten. This
was unusual, it being Worsley's almost invariable
custom to get up much earlier and come down to
breakfast at nine.*" Here was food for thought.
In the first place, the evidence (if reliable)
helped, though only to a limited extent, in
determining the time of the death. Hitherto,
Worsley had been last seen at about half-past
nine ; now it became clear that he had been
alive some forty minutes later, though still

while they were all in the drawing-room, still before Halliford went out to make sure about the gate. Why had Leyland wanted that piece of information hushed up? Probably because he wanted the court to think that the death might have occurred while there was still a little daylight left, still a theoretical chance of finding that lost pipe in the silo. Anyhow, there it was. By the way, which side of the house did Worsley's room look out? To be sure, it looked out towards the river; its light, therefore, would not have been visible from the front at the time when the other lights were visible from the front, just before the race started.

But there was another point raised by the footman's disclosure. Worsley had expected, for some reason, to be sitting up specially late that night. It might mean nothing; it might mean that he was desperately anxious to finish his article before he went to bed; it might mean he had determined to wait up for the elopers, when they should return, and share their sandwiches. But there was just the suggestion that Worsley had plans of his own; and that these involved, not a casual stroll (or climb) but a considerable expedition. What such an expedition could be baffled the imagination. Here was a man whose life was ordinarily mapped out on a regular plan; who had neither low tastes nor any real love of excitement – why should he have contemplated these mysterious movements on the one night when he knew he was to be alone in the house ? Or, take it another way – if you assumed that he had the intention of suicide, had he anything to gain by postponing the hour at which he would be called in the morning ? Not, surely, if he intended to kill himself in the silo ; it was clear that his body would be found in any case soon after daybreak. Bredon confessed himself at a loss. Could he take Mrs. Halliford into consultation ? Hardly ; the documents Leyland had handed to him were meant to be confidential and they must not go beyond Angela at the furthest.

There was even later, though purely negative, evidence to be had about Worsley's movements. It appeared that Mrs. Halliford, who scarcely shared the general excitement about the race because she knew already that she was to be the heroine of it, determined to make the best use of the half-hour between the general retirement and the start. Accordingly she had summoned her maid, and both of them were engaged in affairs of the wardrobe up till the moment of Mrs. Halliford's departure. The maid went downstairs at about ten minutes past eleven, when all the eloping party had disappeared, and she was prepared to swear that the door of the library was open when she passed it and the room in darkness. In the course of the hour that elapsed between 10.10 and 11.10, Worsley had left the library. It was possible that he was in his bedroom when the hue and cry began, but it was not likely that he had waited long in his bedroom – all the indications pointed to a brief and businesslike visit. Probably, then, he had left the house either before the eloping race started or not much later. This information had been produced at the inquest, but the bearing of it had not been evident to the general public, and the coroner had not stressed it.

Finally, there was the article on which the ill-fated gentleman had been engaged on the last evening of his life. It dealt with the position of natives in South Africa, a subject which, Bredon remembered, the writer had been discussing earlier in the day with Carberry, who became almost inarticulate with rage over it. He had left off at the end of a sentence but not, clearly, at the end of a paragraph, and the final words had been blotted, not allowed to dry of themselves. That should mean, for choice, one thing and one thing only – that Worsley had laid down his pen, not because he meant to retire for the night at that moment, but because he found it was time for him to fulfil some other engagement. He was not actually called away in a great hurry, or he would hardly have blotted it ; but the action was not final. It had been his intention to finish up that paragraph, if he had time, before he went to bed.

BREDON WAS STILL sitting at the writing-table in his bedroom, scowling at the contradictory sheets of manuscript, when his wife came in and found him. " I haven't half been looking for you," she announced. " Been going through the silo with a fine-tooth comb, or what? Sholto's been ringing you."

Sholto meant the offices of the Indescribable. " What did I tell Leyland just now? The moment they find out there's publicity in the show they let it rip, and don't want any confidential reports. Good, then we can start for home when we like. I'm sick of this muddle."

Actually, he was in two minds. He had not really bred out his human instinct of curiosity ; did not really like, any more than most of us, to leave a problem unsolved. But he posed – and the pose had almost become a part of his nature – as one who had only taken on the profession of a " spy " under protest because there was no other way of making a living ; and accordingly he felt it a duty whenever he was told not to inquire further into a case to force himself into an attitude of grateful relief. On this occasion he had spoken too soon.

" Nothing of that kind, you poor dear. They want you to go up there and interview somebody ; somebody terribly important, but they won't say who. A man, I'm glad to say ; I got that out of Sholto before I consented to let you go. But he's got to see you to-morrow."

" Well, let him come here and see me."

" I thought of that, but he's not that kind of person at all. His medals and things would all come unstuck if he took to going about England and seeing people. They have to come and see him."

" Blast his medals. How's the car running ? "

" Not too well, since that King's Norton joy ride ; I thought of having her vetted. But there's a capital train at 10.10, and you can have your interview at 3 – they say that'll be all right – and catch the 4.45 back here. I thought I'd take you in in the morning, you see, and get a garage to give the car the once-over, and then I'd go and look round the cathedral, and have lunch at a tea-shop – why are all cathedral towns so full of tea-shops ? – and bring you back in the evening."

" Looks as if it had got to be done. Have you broken it to the Hallifords ? "

" Yes, that's all right. She was terribly scared at first, because she thought it meant

144

our going away altogether, and who was to look after poor Walter? Poor Walter, indeed – she's got her eye on you, that woman. But when she heard you'd be coming back she was all smiles again. Oo, I wish I knew what it was all about."

Privately, Bredon felt fairly certain that the mysterious interview was connected with the problem he already had in hand, not the preface to a new one. And that problem continued to occupy his mind all through the weary miles of his London journey. The bright lawn and its tea-tables, with the sprawling terraces of flowers beckoning you down to the river ; the drive populous with the flare of motor-lamps ; the grey light of early day stealing down the fantastic perspective of the silo till it rested on what lay beneath ; the hot scented paths of the kitchen-garden, whose stones he had examined so narrowly in search of enlightenment – these were the scenes that dominated his imagination, these were outlined for him on the dull oblong of the carriage-window. He did not see, or saw only as an unregarded background, the fruit-trees of Pershore flashing past him in vistas, and revolving as they flashed, the thick weed-tufts stemming the channels of Evenlode, the ghastly brick panorama of Oxford taken in extension, Dorchester Clump and the Downs, and the Thames with its secret islands, and those grim last stages of the journey which speak to the jaded traveller only of biscuits and milk.

I have written elsewhere of the Indescribable building, and how well it represents that period of our national architecture which finds its inspiring motive in the resolution to avoid paying super-tax. For Bredon, as an official of the Company, it was not necessary to waste time in the gilded dalliance of the great palm court, or have his name bandied about in whispers by the sleek attendants. He passed through familiar corridors, exchanging a word here and there with acquaintances ; and the giant clock (designed to recall the uncertainties of human life by depicting the Twelve Labours of Hercules) barely stood at half-past three when he found himself closeted with one of the five really important people in the office and a polite, mysterious stranger. " Ah, Bredon, that you ? Can I introduce you . . ." The stranger held up a deprecating hand : " No names, perhaps, if you don't mind. Glad you were able to come, Mr. Bredon," and, when they were alone together, " It is really very good of you, most good of you." He was of the military caste ; you did not need to be a detective to make sure of that, in spite of his civilian dress. Bredon, who had had much experience of the type during the War, wrote him down without hesitation as a brass hat. But the directness and simplicity which we like to recognise as part of the military character was overlaid, here, with something subtler and more elaborate. The man, you felt, was trying to be sinister; he was of that strange cross-breed which we designate – by oxymoron, some think – as " Military Intelligence."

" I have heard a good deal about you, Mr. Bredon, from an old friend of mine, Colonel Gullett. You served with him, I think? A fine soldier. He used to say it was a pity we didn't manage to keep you on in uniform. However, I understand from what I've been hearing just now that you've been finding an outlet for your talents with the Indescribable. Smart company. You are representing them at the moment, I think, down at Lastbury? "

" One moment, sir, perhaps I ought to make that clearer. I represent the Company on demand ; they have a right, I mean, to call on my services at any time. But on this occasion I have had no orders from them ; I simply happened to be staying with the family at Lastbury, in a friendly way, when all this trouble happened."

" In a friendly way – dear me ! That makes things rather less plain sailing. Still, there are duties which have a tantamount claim on us as citizens, don't you agree ? Policeman tells you

147

to help him collar a thief, you *got* to help him ; that's the law, ain't it ? Well, here the situation's not much different. What I mean is, I hope we can count on your co-operation, Mr. Bredon, in these rather delicate circumstances. You know as well as I do that we're not satisfied with the coroner's verdict ; it was only meant to satisfy the public ; you know that. But it doesn't satisfy *us* ; and when I say that, I must ask you not to be inquisitive about what I mean by *us*. There's more in the machinery of government than meets the eye ; you know that, of course. Intelligent man. Now, what I want to get at is, Can we count on you ? "

Bredon found himself in the position most of us know all too well – that in which you long for two separate faculties of attention, one to register and answer with, another to store up golden memories of the interview for subsequent farmyard imitation. This man was going to be good value, there was no doubt ; as a type he was infinitely worth studying ; on the other hand, some effort must be made to look impressed and to answer the call respectfully. At the same time, he saw the old difficulty looming ahead : how far could you reconcile the duties of a spy with those of a gentleman ?

" I hope I should always be ready to do anything in the way of assisting justice," he said guardedly. " I mean, if it were a question

148

of making an arrest or anything of that sort. But . . . perhaps you'd explain more definitely what it is you have in mind ? "

" Quite right ; much best that we should be frank with one another. No harm ever came of frankness yet. Let's put it this way ; d'you believe, yourself, that the death of this feller Worsley was an accident ? "

" I haven't been able to construct any picture of the circumstances which could have led to an accident of that sort. And I can't say the Coroner helped me much. What I mean is——"

" That's all right, don't say another word—you don't think it was an accident, that's clear. Now, tell me this – do you think the poor chap committed suicide ? Took his own life ? "

" That's rather a more difficult question to answer. I'd never met Worsley before, you see ; and it's hard to judge the question of suicide without knowing your man. But I didn't, personally, see anything in his manner just before it happened which would have made me guess there was any danger of such a thing happening. And I confess that it doesn't seem to me a natural way for a man to commit suicide : the chances of death were too uncertain."

" I see what you mean ; yes, certainly. You're quite right to be guarded in your statements, of course ; but I can quite see you *don't* think he committed suicide. Very well

149

then, where do we stand ? Where do we stand now, Mr. Bredon ? Here's a man, a public figure, whose loss will be very much felt ; you must take it from me, Mr. Bredon, that his loss will be felt in the very highest quarters. Nobody has any private grudge against him ; his name's never been connected with any woman's. Nobody has any expectations from him, nobody's prospects are endangered by his existence. And then " – the stranger found in a sudden flick of the fingers the only appropriate conclusion to his outburst of rhetoric.

" You're suggesting, sir, that it must be a murder because it seems unlikely that he could have died in any other way ; and that the murder must have been a political one because it seems hard to find any other motive for it. There's rather a lot of *must* about that, isn't there ? I mean, was there any independent reason to expect a political murder of this kind ? Had his life been threatened, for example ? "

" My dear Mr. Bredon, you may take it from me that the people who are sharp enough to execute these political murders are sharp enough to do it when there's no *independent reason* to expect it. If we always waited till there were threatening letters – oh no, it won't do, that, won't do at all." He spoke as if Bredon had been desperately searching for a sophistical evasion of plain facts.

150

" I only meant – well sir, I don't want to press that. But now, you talk of ' these political murders ' as if there had been a series of them ; is it fair to ask what group this murder – if it is a murder, and a political murder – falls into ? I mean, it might be possible, mightn't it, to reconstruct what happened by comparing it with parallel cases ? "

" Mr. Bredon, you may take it from me that the people who are sharp enough to execute these political murders are sharp enough to do it in a different way every time. And another thing – don't believe all you see in the papers. These newspaper fellers – well, there's no harm done, but don't believe everything you read. No, we've got to investigate this case as if it stood entirely by itself, see ? Entirely by itself."

" Well, in that case, perhaps it would be best to put it like this : I am inclined to think there's been foul play, and, if in the course of my stay at Lastbury I find that impression confirmed, I'll do my best to follow up the question, in the interests of justice generally. Whether there was a political motive behind it all is no business of mine ; and even if there is, that is not likely to help me in my inquiries. Shall we put it like that ? "

" Ah, but pardon me, the political motive may have a distinct bearing on the case. The

human equation comes in, you see, doesn't it ?
A foreigner, for example, is more worth suspecting in a case of this kind than a Britisher ;
a Socialist – you will see that I'm being very
frank with you, Mr. Bredon – may be more
worth suspecting than a man who has a stake
in the country. That's why I thought it might
be worth while to have this little chat, just to
indicate one or two lines of inquiry which you
might have overlooked. Well, we can count
on you, then, to act for us ? "

" I'm afraid that's putting it rather strongly,
sir. You can count on me to help justice
forward, if I come to the conclusion that murder
has been done and that the murderer's getting
away with it. But I can't very well act as
anybody's representative while I allow my
host and hostess to think that I'm merely
stopping on as their guest. I mean, there are
decencies——"

" Oh, my dear Mr. Bredon, no ; please don't
suppose that, for a moment ! Of course you
must go entirely by what you feel to be fitting
in the circumstances. All we wanted was to be
quite certain how we stood ; and, believe me,
from our point of view this interview has been
quite satisfactory, most satisfactory. And I
think I can safely say that, if you do help us to
fix our suspicions in the right quarter, your
services will not be forgotten. Your train,

yes, don't let me keep you ; it was really most kind of you to come."

" More than eight hours in this beastly train," said Bredon to himself ; " and all to delude that old poop into the idea that he's done an afternoon's work. What was his great word? Oh, yes, *tantamount*. That makes it almost worth while."

THERE WERE WORSE ways of spending that day, however, than sitting in a train. The early morning had been indistinguishable from that of yesterday, which proved to be a day of breathless stuffiness ; from that of the day before, which was one of oppressive heat. But this time the mist, instead of dispersing as the morning wore on, closed in and acquired substance ; before long it had turned into a roaring deluge of rain – rain of the Welsh border, that turns the world into a sobbing wilderness of wet. Leyland, camping out in his ridiculous little tent just upstream from Last-bury, caught the effect of it full. It must be supposed that the genuine camper has tricks of his own for dealing with days of pitiless rain such as this was, or else his consciousness of virtue provides him with an oleaginous front to meet the storm. It is certain that Leyland, who was a mere impostor in his present sur-roundings, was left resourceless. However tightly you gripped the canvas superstructure about you, it only developed fresh vents and creases, through which runnels of water emptied themselves on you unawares. He tried the boathouse close by, though he had to trespass in order to do it ; but this, too, had a porous roof, and he feared discovery if he should creep under the huge tarpaulin sheet that guarded the motor-boat inside. In despair, he struck across country for the village and for the minute public house from which he was wont to supply himself with necessaries.

A village there was, attached to Lastbury, though it was hard to see how it ever came there, for it was clearly older than the bridge, and, having no ford within two miles either way, it can have enjoyed little commerce with the more populous side of the river. Yet there were two or three straggling cottages, their moss-grown thatch crying out for repair, with little gardens, sloping down crazily towards the river, full of hollyhocks and spreading nasturtium. There was a tiny church, served at intervals in these lean days, but once, presumably, calculated to provide a whole Vicar with pulpit and living ; and, more important for our immediate purpose, there was a low, ivy-covered, ramshackle public house, the Grapes by dedication, which maintained its license somehow, though it had a perpetual air of solitude and neglect. It was not a great deal of consolation that he enjoyed here, even when they had lit a fire for him in the bar parlour, which was also the bar and the private room. Such rooms in small country inns are always full of mysterious doors, which lead to crazy stairs and to stone passages smelling of soap ; through these the dampness of the outer air crept in and chilled the veins. Nor was there a great deal of intellectual entertainment to be derived from the ornaments of the room – two shepherdesses on the mantelpiece, with a burden of dead bulrushes, some German oleographs representing small, half-naked children being run away with in goat-carriages, a certificate of aggregation to the Ancient Order of Buffaloes, and a very old-fashioned musical-box which did not play.

It was better, though, than the tent ; and the approach of noon brought two further consolations. He would be able to order a drink for himself, and the same natural instinct would, little doubt of it, draw one or two of the male population innwards, for company and perhaps for information. Leyland did not despise any source of evidence, and it was a favourite principle of his – " a comfortable doctrine " his friends called it – that hanging round in bars was never time wasted for a detective. The Hallifords, as Bredon had pointed out, were the kind of people who do not really belong to the countryside, of whose ways and habits, therefore, the countryside knows little. But at least their rustic neighbours would have caught some touch of their quality ; it was not improbable that men employed on the estate would be among those present, nay, men employed on the working of the silo. Local opinion on local happenings was always valuable ; there might be local information, too, about people's movements. So far, everybody had assumed that if murder had been done, somebody living in the house was responsible for it. That was probable enough ; in this very remote corner of the world it was hardly likely that the guest of a day would come across an enemy. But Worsley, it was to be remembered, had visited the district before ; there was just the chance of a rural vendetta. No harm, anyhow, in discovering whether any strangers had been seen about on the night of the tragedy or the day before it.

It was not long before he was joined by two *habitués* of the establishment. One was a baker's assistant, going his leisurely round on horseback ; the other, he guessed, a ditcher or a stone-breaker, who spent a good deal of his time ruminating on life without reaching any very sensational conclusions. Both looked at Leyland rather distrustfully ; the days are gone by when every holiday-maker, however roughly dressed, took rank as a gentleman, and

157

this half drenched figure in shorts was difficult to place. Leyland, however, greeted them with conventional politeness and did not seek to obtrude further conversation on them ; soon they began to talk across him in high pitched Herefordshire voices ; and he had no sooner grown acclimatised to their speech than he found they were talking about events at Lastbury.

The findings of the coroner's jury did not seem to have produced any conviction locally. On an evening so full of events, of the coming and going of motor-cars, you do not (rustic shrewdness argued) expect anything so tame as suicide, let alone accidental death. Murder there had undoubtedly been ; and if the jury had decided otherwise, that was because people like them up at Halliford's knew how to put themselves on the right side of the law. Leyland found himself wondering at the tradition, centuries old perhaps in these parts, that in the eye of the law carriage folks could do no wrong ; they were not taken and hanged in Hereford jail as Tom, Dick, or Harry would be. At the same time, those alehouse critics were not quite unconscious of the change that had come over England, the change from aristocracy to oligarchy, from carriage folks to motor folks. They realised that the Hallifords belonged to a flashy sort of world, whose " goings-on " could best be understood in the light of the cinema. It was a matter of course that there must be sordid intrigues in a house where cocktails were drunk and people stayed in bed for breakfast.

Nor was there any hesitation in the mind of Mr. Jackson (the ditcher or stone-breaker) about the identity of the culprits. The Hallifords, husband and wife, had put away their guest, you could see that easily, couldn't you ? Nobody else would have thought of shutting a man up in the silo to suffocate him there ; nobody else would have been powerful enough to suppress the activities of the police. As for the motive, Mr. Jackson's theories were plain but unprintable. So resolute were his suspicions that Leyland felt he would have been half carried away by them if it had not been for the evidence resting in his pocket at the moment ; evidence which proved that Worsley's death meant financial disaster to the Hallifords and that both of them were quite well aware of that beforehand. This was not knowledge, however, which could be shared with his present company ; and he looked admiringly at Mr. Jackson, occasionally echoing the " Ah ! " with which the baker's assistant acknowledged the profundity of his thought.

On one point, very deferentially, he did manage to side-track the orator. Would it be possible, now, for someone to have got into

Lastbury that night from the outside, who could tell us a good deal more about what had happened if we could lay hands on him ? This was not merely a random guess of his. It was clear to him that, if Tollard's story were true, a stranger must have passed close to the house that night. For Tollard's breakdown had been on the road which made for Lastbury Bridge and for that destination only ; Tollard, by his own account, had had to empty out his petrol and get a fresh supply from a passing car which had been coming from the Hereford direction. Or did he say a lorry ? Anyhow, the driver of that vehicle, starting a little ahead of Tollard, must have crossed the bridge and climbed the hill to a point only a few hundred yards from the Lastbury gate. Mr. Jackson did not think much of this suggestion. It wasn't often a car passed that way at all, late at night, without it would be going to Lastbury Manor ; and as for a lorry, that bridge wasn't built for heavy traffic, and there was a notice on it saying what the fine was for driving lorries over it, as Leyland would see for himself any time he liked to cast an eye over it.

At half-past twelve the outer door swung open and there was a fresh accession to the party who made his salutes. Asked where was George then, he explained that George had been to doctor and doctor had told he he had a gastric stomach, that was how it was. The newcomer proved not only to be a worker at the silo, but the identical John Hookway who had first sighted the corpse. It may easily be imagined how this fact enhanced his entertainment value ; how firmly Leyland had to suppress his policeman's instinct of cross-examination and let the hero of the occasion tell his story in his own interminable way. He spent a great deal of time in retailing to his audience facts which were already familiar to them ; a great deal more in searching for, and rejecting as inadequate, various similes which would illustrate his immediate reactions on seeing the corpse. But, just when Leyland was despairing of getting any value for his money, Mr. Hookway began on a fresh, subsidiary saga, dealing with the extraordinary behaviour of his pitchfork.

Pitchforks, it appeared, had to be taken back to the farm when work was over, not left about at or in the silo. Such were the orders of Mr. Sturt, the foreman, who (it was facetiously surmised) was afraid they would take a chill if they were left out. On the evening before the murder work, as we know, left off rather earlier than usual, because there was no more of the crop left to carry. And Mr. Hookway had some mysterious business, it seemed, which took him in the opposite direction from the farm and indeed to the further side of the bridge.

The nature of this business was hinted at it with much allusive patois and many anxious glances in Leyland's direction, from which he inferred that it was probably a poaching expedition of some kind, probably on the river bank. Be that as it may, the pitchfork was left leaning against the wall of the silo, not just outside the hatches, look you, but a good half of the way round. Hookway's idea was to pick it up as he returned from the river and carry it with him to the farm, which was more or less on his way home. But when he got back to the silo it had been removed ; and at first he thought there would be trouble, because it would be like Mr. Sturt's way to carry it back to the farm himself. Then, to his surprise, he saw that it had not travelled far after all ; he caught sight of it leaning against the wall *inside* the silo, about two feet away from the hatches. He concluded that somebody from the house, Mr. Halliford himself as like as not, for he would often come down that way of an evening, had stowed the thing away inside for fear it should be stolen. Mr. Hookway by now was heavily loaded, he did not say with what, but Leyland deduced that he had a salmon concealed about his person ; he was disinclined to scramble up the hatches, and not particularly anxious to undergo the scrutiny of the farm. So with one thing and another he decided to leave the pitchfork where it was. It would be an easy business to be up ahead of Mr. Sturt next morning and remove it from the silo before it was noticed.

So far was so good. But next morning, when he was the first to arrive on the scene, his emotions were once more beyond the range of metaphor when he discovered that the fork was standing exactly where he had left it at five o'clock the evening before, and that there was no fork standing just inside the trap, as there had been at about eight o'clock on the evening before. It was touch and go whether he did not climb up the hatches then and there to make sure, in which case, as he pointed out, he would have come across the dead man's body at close quarters and fainted and fallen off the steps as likely as not. Instead of which, he adopted the pitchfork without further question at the time, and it was only when he came to climb up the ladder later on, to make the trap ready, that he saw the dead man's body from up there at the top – and this was the signal for Mr. Hookway to plunge into his original story again and tell it all over from the beginning.

It cannot be said that the symposium at the Grapes did much to unravel this fresh piece of mystery. The theory, adduced by the baker's assistant, that some person or persons unknown had " chivvied " Worsley into the silo at the end of a pitchfork and shut him up there,

163

seemed on the whole to win the approval of the company. Leyland felt that more concentrated thought was needed to elucidate the subject ; and, noticing at the same time that the rain had spent most of its fury, made his way back to his old quarters. It had cleared altogether when, later that afternoon, a motor-hearse crossed Lastbury Bridge at the decorous pace of fifteen miles an hour, carrying the remains of Cecil Worsley to the place of burning appointed for them.

THE PITCHFORK, LEYLAND decided, must be left over till he could discuss it with Bredon. The whole incident looked as if, somehow, it must be in line with those other odd appearances and disappearances which Bredon himself had noted in the walled garden. Also, it was too theoretical a problem, too tenuous a clue, for Leyland's taste; he preferred the rough and tumble of detection. And there *was* another new line to be followed up – the whole business of Tollard's alibi. Quite certainly, Tollard's depositions before the police were worth verifying. By his own account, he had only gone a mile or so from the gate on the night of the murder when he developed engine trouble. He was a fairly good mechanic, and he tried every possible means of dealing with the situation until finally he was reduced to the supposition that some water must have got into his petrol tank. He had filled up from a can at Lastbury, not from a pump; and defective cans had been heard of before now. He set himself to empty his tank, resigned to

165

missing the race and only concerned to get the car back to its garage. He had no spare petrol ; unless a casual passer-by intervened to rescue him he must wait till the return of the other competitors. So far, his story sounded good enough. From that point onwards (as Herodotus would say) the accounts are by no means agreed.

According to his own story, a lorry – it *was* a lorry – passed soon after midnight, fortunately with some petrol on board, which he bought off the man, thus managing to return to Lastbury at about a quarter past twelve. According to Phyllis Morel's story, he was still there when she came by at about twenty-five minutes past twelve ; he signalled, but she refused to slacken speed for fear he might be a motor bandit. The good Samaritan, then, whoever it was, could not really have passed Tollard till some time after that ; and it was not till a quarter to one that she heard him garaging his car – or thought so. A story already weakened by this conflict of testimony was now further called in question by internal evidence. Mr. Jackson had not been at fault ; on casting his eye over the bridge Leyland saw a notice, prominent enough, which forbade the transit of lorries. Conceivably some driver, strange to the district, might have taken that road in ignorance. But it sounded more as if Tollard's whole story was an invention ; nothing was certain about his movements or those of his car after he fell out of the race, except Phyllis Morel's evidence, which he strenuously denied – that he and it were on the road, a mile out of Lastbury, about twenty-five minutes after midnight.

How his story was to be tested did not readily appear. The Hallifords kept no chauffeur ; it was an odd man about the house who did what cleaning was necessary at the garage ; and he, like the rest, had gone off on the motor-boat expedition that night. Advertising for the driver of a probably mythical lorry was not likely to yield any useful result. Should he proceed by way of reconstruction, pouring water into Tollard's petrol tank, and then cadging a ride off him to see what his reactions would be when the same old trouble set in ? On the whole, no ; his chance introduction to Tollard was too useful to be squandered in such a fashion. Should he secure an official accomplice from Hereford, who would pose as the driver of the lorry, interview Tollard, and complain with polite firmness that a bad shilling had been paid him in return for his petrol ?   It would be easy to lay hands on an accomplice and a bad shilling, but such methods would certainly warn Tollard, if guilty, that he was being watched ; if innocent, he might make trouble over the imposture. Of course, it was possible to question the local police about late-travelling cars on the night in question ; not on the Hereford side of the river, where the eloping race would have fouled all traces, but on the further side of Lastbury. If Tollard really got petrol from a passing lorry, that lorry ought to be traceable. . . .

Come to think of it, there was another side to all this. If Tollard was telling the truth, then not one but two strange cars had gone past, that night, in the neighbourhood of Lastbury. There was the car or lorry which had helped Tollard out, but there was also the car which had hailed Phyllis Morel as she passed, about ten minutes later. And that car, it seemed probable, must have stopped at Lastbury, or close to it, or *why did Phyllis imagine she heard Tollard garaging his car at* 12.45 ? Tollard's alibi must be investigated, not merely to make certain what Tollard was up to, but to make certain that there was not a strange visitor to Lastbury after all. In despair of a solution, Leyland made a pilgrimage, towards evening, to the spot where, according to the story, Tollard's car had been held up. It would be something to have a " composition of place " ; there was the outside chance that the inmates of some neighbouring cottage, on that night of motoring activity, might have been kept awake and have preserved memories. In this last hope he was disappointed. The " turn in the road, close to a big haystack at the end of a wood," was recognisable beyond all doubt, and there was no cottage within hooting distance of it. No need to question the loneliness of the place at night, so quiet it seemed now in the broad daylight. Nothing seemed to stir in the deep woods or stray across their wide drives ; no human figure was to be seen working in the fields or trudging along the grass lanes that skirted them ; only the drip from the leaves and the gurgling of little runnels by the side of the road seemed to break the stillness. Yes, it was the kind of spot you would choose if you were anxious, for purposes of your own, to fall out in a midnight race and to stage a casual breakdown. And the kind of spot which, motoring past at the same hour, you might easily take for the lurking place of high-way robbers. It would be easy for one man to stand in the road and have confederates hidden behind a thriving hedge like that. Or was there a drop behind the hedge ? It was in gratifying his curiosity on so trivial a point that Leyland made a discovery which more than requited the effort of his walk. Lying in a thick bed of nettles, where it had been tossed, evidently, over the hedge from the road, was an empty petrol can, its colours still bright, its

169

metal work unrusted. Blessings on the meticulous traditions of mass production ! It bore a registration number on its under side. And with that number carefully docketed in his note-book, Leyland made his way to the nearest telephone call-box, at the junction with the main Hereford road. That was the advantage of being a policeman ; you had behind you an infinitely painstaking machinery which would trace one out of a million petrol cans, find out where it was first filled, how it changed hands, what garage supplied it to whom. Bredon couldn't do a thing like that.

As he trudged back to his encampment, he turned over in his mind the possibilities of the suspicion which now exercised him. If it proved that Tollard had lied at his examination before the police, if that meant that Tollard was guilty of, or at least privy to, the murder, how were you going to reconstruct his actions ? His breakdown had evidently been a mere pretence ; little fear that the Arnolds or the Carberrys would embarrass him with offers of help when they were going all out in a race with money on it. He must have supposed that the rest of the party would be away for several hours ; he could hardly have foreseen Phyllis Morel's early return. But it was evidently safer to do what he had to do at once : you had to allow for the possibility of accident. Tollard,

then, would turn his car round as soon as the
last echoes of the hunt had died away ; would
make straight for the end of the drive, would
probably walk from there, to avoid disturbing
the sleep of servants in the house. By now, it
would be about half past eleven, not much
later. He may have expected to find that
Worsley, an early bed-goer in an empty house,
would have turned in already ; instead, it
would seem that he was actually in his bedroom,
beginning to undress – the evidence favoured
that view. The same evidence made it impossible to believe that there had been a struggle
in the bedroom ; Worsley must have been
induced, under some pretext, to come out for a
stroll, or perhaps to help overcome some
imaginary refractoriness about the car. At any
rate, it is only a short expedition that is proposed ; Worsley does not bother to take his
watch with him, or even his eyeglass. They
walk together to the car ; possibly Worsley
is induced to bend down and examine something. Then – perhaps a chloroform pad first
of all ; a struggle in which the victim bursts a
collar-stud, tears his clothes a little, fails to
fight off his assailant. Then smothering, with
cushions from the car or whatever else came
handy ; then the careful disposal of the body.
Possibly it had to be hoisted up through the
hatches ; possibly the pulley, stiff as it was, was

171

called into requisition, and the dead body first pulled up on to the platform and then dropped down onto the soft floor of ensilage. All that need not have taken long ; perhaps half an hour at the outside. Midnight at latest.

What would be his next step ? Evidently to establish as good an alibi as possible. And here, Leyland had to admit, something must have gone extremely wrong. Tollard would have had no alibi if he had confessed to meeting Phyllis Morel at 12.25 ; he had still less if he claimed to have been in the house by 12.15. He had no proof how long his breakdown had delayed him, except that of an alleged lorry-driver whom he had never offered to produce. By waiting for the return of the elopers, he would have had some sort of testimony to his movements ; though in that case the interval would have been so long that a continued vigil by the roadside would have seemed improbable. Perhaps you could work it out something like this – he did not reckon on the extreme loneliness of the road and imagined that, quite soon after midnight, he would be able to stop a passing car and have proof that he was a mile away from Lastbury. The minutes lengthened out, and still nobody passed ; then, at 12.25, he saw Phyllis Morel's headlights. He did not imagine that any of the Lastbury party could be back yet ; assumed, therefore, that it was a

strange car and tried to flag the occupant.
The car, however, simply put on speed and
vanished ; it was useless to him as evidence,
so he went home disappointed ; and, finding that
nothing beyond his bare word could be produced
in evidence, put the date of his return at 12.15.
It was a poor alibi, but as long as he liked to
stick to it that he was tinkering his car from
11.10 to 12.10, the jury would have to give him
the benefit of the doubt.

It was fortunate that the police interrogation
had been so prompt ; that no time had been
allowed for the members of the house-party to
concoct a story between them. For Tollard,
not realising that it was Phyllis Morel who
passed him on the road, had falsified the timing
of his movements, and Phyllis Morel had
unwittingly given him away. Again Leyland
wondered at the inadequacy of the alibi arrangements. To create the impression that he had
spent a long time trying to repair the car,
Tollard had evidently emptied out the petrol
in good earnest and filled up from a can he
carried with him ; that, probably, to-morrow's
information from police headquarters would
make abundantly clear. But if he, Leyland,
could find out any positive traces which would
connect Tollard with the murder, the flimsy
pretexts would be blown away under the most
cursory investigation. . . . Well, well, it was

fortunate criminals were not a hundred per cent. brains.

A car came up behind him, slowed down and threw open a door for him. It was the Bredons returning from Hereford. Leyland grinned a good deal at the recital of the mysterious interview, and admitted that, though the police chiefs, thank God, were cleverer than the public gave them credit for, once you touched the secret service you must be prepared for what you got. In return, he described his own day, with severe comments on the climate of Hereford-shire, the wisdom of those who regarded camping out as a form of enjoyment, and the luck of those who had nice red brick houses to stay in and servants to bring them early morning tea. He retailed, too, the local gossip, and asked Bredon whether he really had no suspicions of a man who claimed to have filled up with petrol from a lorry on a road on which lorries were not allowed. He did not mention his further discovery in the hedge ; he wanted to make sure how that panned out before he gave himself any credit for it. But he repeated the saga of the pitchfork and found he had made a hit with this. Bredon looked very grave, and his brows knitted in bewilderment. " That's the devil and all," he said, " that pitchfork. I hate it when it looks as if quite impossible things had been happening. And I don't see

174

how this points to anything but the impossible. Not that, of course, I'm really interested. But it was kind of you to lend me those notes, all the same."

WHILE BREDON HAD been closeted with the giant brain, and Leyland had been hobnobbing with the great heart of the people, Angela too had had an interview and improved an acquaintance. Looking round cathedrals makes a great hole in your time when you are simply rushing through; when you are trying to cheat the hours of waiting, it is curiously inadequate. She saw Miles off soon after ten; by half past eleven she felt she knew the cathedral by heart, and had to fall back on the other amenities, not too numerous, of an old-fashioned town. By the time she selected her tea-shop and sat down to luncheon she was in a mood for welcoming any company fortune might send her. And fortune was kind; she found herself sitting opposite Phyllis Morel, who had come into Hereford, it appeared, to answer the charge of breaking the speed-limits of her country.

The fine inflicted by the magistrates did not seem to have had any remedial effect; she was frankly unconvinced by their point of view.

176

" It's such rot," she said, " when you compare the mock trial I had to-day with that inquest up at Lastbury. You'd think, wouldn't you, that the death of a man who had his portrait in all the weekly papers was a thing to worry about and make a great song and dance over ; whereas the speed knocked out of her auto by the woman Morel was a comparatively trifling affair ? Not a bit of it, my dear. Up at Lastbury, they hardly listened to a word any of the witnesses said, and the attitude of that silly old coroner was simply that the thing mustn't happen again ; as if it was likely to ! Whereas my speed-driving is a thing that is very likely to happen again ; indeed, it's going to, but they didn't seem to mind about that ; vengeance on the woman Morel was all they cared about. She must be made to suffer by parting with a large quantity of the stuff ; whereas if a party of thugs had done in poor Cecil Worsley, as that fool of a paper suggested, they'd have got away with it all right, wouldn't they ? I say, what heavenly coffee ! "

" That's what my husband always says," agreed Angela. " He says the law nowadays takes no interest either in justice or in morals, and if you went down Piccadilly with no clothes on at all you would simply be run in for obstructing the traffic. I suppose the police feel that a hushed up murder does less harm to

177

public discipline than the possibility of a motor smash. But you know, I don't think that inquest was quite typical. I've been at these shows before and I've generally had the impression that the coroner hoped it would be a murder because it meant more publicity for him."

" And of course it justifies his existence, same as an insurance company paying up a claim. One's always told they like doing it, though I must say they manage to conceal their pleasure pretty well when I come across them. Oh, I forgot. Perhaps I oughtn't to have said that."

" Bless you, there's no loyalty to the old firm about Miles and me ; you can say what you like. As a matter of fact, the Indescribable is so odiously rich that I think it does really like paying ; a sort of glow of munificence, don't you know, when it coughs up ten thousand, like an uncle tipping his nephew at school. But I suppose justifying one's own existence is the reason why most people do most things, except the people who have a real love of interference. Did *you* think there was anything in that article – about the thugs, I mean ? "

" Good God no ; it was only meant to make our flesh creep. It's funny the way the word *murder* still does that, when we've come to take most other things so calmly. Why should murder be so wrong ? We've all got to die, and there are very few crimes that would bring more happiness to mankind, if judiciously applied, of course."

" That's just the point, surely, it's cheating ; using force to do the puzzle. One knows lots of people who've *killed* people ; in the War, for example, or in accidents with cars. But murder's different ; it takes a mean advantage of the situation. The murderer just disqualifies himself ; that's how I feel."

" You feel as strongly as all that ? Tell me, if you thought a person was quite possibly a murderer, though not certainly, what would you feel about him ? Could you marry him, for example ? "

Angela's head whirled for a moment. Then she remembered (1) that nobody so far, except Leyland, had thought of connecting Tollard with the murder, (2) that Tollard had been mixed up in a murder trial long ago, (3) that Phyllis Morel wouldn't know that Angela knew this, (4) that quite possibly Phyllis wasn't thinking about Tollard in that way at all. But she felt she had changed colour, ever so slightly, and that she ought to cover her tracks. " I'm being worried," she said, " by that feeling of having done something before. You know the kind of thing I mean, Wordsworth's Intimations and all that. Have I or have I not, in this life and during my waking moments, been asked

179

whether I could bring myself to marry a murderer ? . . . No, I've got it! I was once asked by
a young man, who would have liked to pretend
to be a bit in love with me, whether I thought
he was a murderer, and if so whether I didn't
mind sitting there talking to him ? As a
matter of fact, I did a good deal ; not because I
thought he was a murderer, but because he had
such a dreadfully Oxford voice. As far as I
remember, I annoyed him by telling him I
didn't think he was the kind of person who
would commit a murder. I wonder, though,
about your question. I should have thought
it all depended on the grounds of the suspicion.
I mean, if it was a man who'd been suspected
of murder because a whole lot of external
circumstances seemed to point to him as the
owner of the blunt instrument, I don't think I'd
worry – assuming he wasn't the *kind* of person
who murders people. But if he'd been suspected of murder because of his character and
antecedents, only they hadn't been able to get a
conviction because of some technical difficulty
about the evidence, then I'd certainly think
twice about it. I should hate to go to bed
feeling that I might be next on the list."

Phyllis Morel stared long and hard at the end
of her coffee-spoon. Then she said, " Yes, but
it isn't so blamed easy to know who would be a
murderer and who wouldn't. A question of

atmospheres, you'll say. But put it in the concrete – Is old Pa Carberry the sort of man who'd commit a murder? "

" He isn't the sort of man one could marry, anyhow," objected Angela. " I mean, he has that dreadful *little woman* manner about him which would always make me want to scream. But I think – yes, I think on the whole he's a starter. Not very charitable really, this conversation, is it? Still, you began it. I should say he's a real he man, a man of actions ; also, he's no illusions about the value of human life – you heard him, didn't you, when he had that crash row with poor Mr. Worsley over the South African natives? And I should say he's a man who thinks very little, so that if he had a grudge on his mind it would work and work and work until he did something dreadful. But I only met him a day or two ago, remember, and he may be a clergyman in lay clothes for all I know."

" Gosh, you're a pretty good judge of character, you know, at short notice."

" Don't you believe it ; Mrs. Bluff the Detective's wife, that's all. Well, your turn ; what about Walter Halliford? "

" Too easy-going, I think. If somebody ran away with his wife, he'd say *My God how annoying*, like the Babu. Come to think of it, if he were a murdering man he'd have got rid of

181

Myrtle long ago. I'm being charitable now, aren't I ? Of course, Myrtle Halliford is kind, or anyhow, as you say, she's fond of interfering with other people. But she's terribly neurotic and a devil when she's roused. I think if Walter did commit a murder, it'd be a simple one : he'd take it all as a matter of course, like shooting a dog that had been running sheep. On the whole, I give him low marks for murder-osity – *and* for marriageability, if it comes to that."

" Yes, I expect you're right. He's direct, though."

" What about Adrian Tollard ? "

Angela's eyes had this rare quality, that they could look at you in a friendly way without seeming to ask inconvenient questions. She looked at Phyllis, but not too long or too hard ; she met eyes that registered either indifference or impudence – there was no frosty resentment in them.

" Mr. Tollard ? I think he's got a cruel mind but not a cruel nature. I can imagine that if you made him dictator he would send quite a lot of people to the guillotine because they didn't agree with his views. He would be carried away by the logic of his own theories and probably make things very uncomfortable for all of us ; some men are like that. And I can just imagine his assassinating somebody on quite abstract grounds if he thought he was a public disaster : acting always as a kind of executioner, you understand. But I don't see him committing a really private murder, I mean one which merely served his own ends or gratified his own feelings. What do *you* think ? "

" I think you're rather taken in by his pose. Men like to be thought less sentimental, more impersonal, than they really are. He'd like to kid you that he's not interested in anything except abstract principles, but when you know him better you find out that he's a mass of romanticism. *I* can imagine his committing a murder in obedience to some private code of honour, from some Quixotic kind of motive, out of chivalry, or one of those feelings he's always pretending he doesn't believe in. I think it would be a rather attractive kind of murder, somehow, and I'm not sure I shouldn't like him better for it."

" That shows what a bad judge of character I really am ; I should never have guessed all that. I think I see what you mean about its being attractive. But then, he's the kind of person one *could* marry."

" Oh Lord yes," said Phyllis, with perhaps a slight overdose of unconcern. " All the same," she added with apparent irrelevance, " one would like to know whether the man one

183

thought of marrying was a murderer or not. Whether you approve or disapprove, it does make a difference. If he's actually committed a murder, it shows he's the kind of person who would ; and then at least one knows something about him."

" Tell me about the Carberrys," put in Angela suddenly. " I mean, do they often come and stay here ? I got the impression, somehow, that they were friends of his rather than of hers ; and yet you'd think she'd have the last word about who comes to stay. The Arnolds one can understand, because they're relations and one has to be polite to relations ; Miles seems to have them everywhere. But I can't quite see why Mrs. Halliford doesn't either like the Carberrys more or ask them less."

" It's bothered me, too," admitted Phyllis. " It's Myrtle that asks the guests, sure thing ; and she was rather particular about whom she asked, though I say it as shouldn't, for fear you might not like them. I've never met them here before, nor heard them talked about much. I think Walter Halliford must have asked them on his own, and then remembered about it too late to unask them. Poor Mrs. Carberry ! She's like a toreador in a china-shop."

" I like Mrs. Carberry, though. It's funny, but that evening, when we were at dinner, she was so cheerful that I thought she must have

184

drawn hare. It was a sitter for the hares, wasn't it ? "

" Oh, I knew Myrtle had won the draw. When you know her better, you can always tell whether things are proceeding according to plan or not. She hates not having things her own way. No, but the person I suspected of being the eloping partner was Cecil Worsley. He seemed in such extraordinary spirits, and bursting with some kind of mystery, if you know what I mean. Of course, I believe *now* that he was meaning all the time to commit suicide and that was the mystery ; the cheerfulness was just put on to take us all in. That's how I read it."

" Oh, you really think it was suicide, do you ? My husband rather thought the gas in the silo wasn't a safe enough way of poisoning yourself ; or that if it was Mr. Worsley wouldn't have known about it."

" Oh, he knew all right. I heard him talking to Walter Halliford about it. Well, we must shout for the bill ; I've got to get back to Last-bury for the funeral. At least, there isn't any funeral really, that's at the other end, but they're taking the coffin away in a motor-hearse. See you this evening."

THE REPLY TO Leyland's inquiries about the
petrol can came through by cipher telegram
early the next morning, which was a Saturday.
He was informed that it had been sent out to
the Ever-open Garages at Golder's Green ;
Proprietor, P. Morel, of whom nothing was
known to the police. It had not been sold,
but it seemed probable that it had been put on
board the proprietor's own car, about a fortnight
ago.

There is such a thing as having our wishes
over-granted. Leyland had been hoping to
trace, through the registration number of the
can, the car, if any, which brought Tollard relief ;
in the alternative, he had hoped to find that
the can was actually on board Tollard's car
all the time and that the story of relief was a
fiction. Now it proved that Tollard had
actually filled up from a can on Phyllis Morel's
car ! And that meant that not only Tollard
was lying, but Phyllis Morel into the bargain ;
that Tollard had established no alibi at all,

186

though he might have appealed to Phyllis; that Phyllis's own word in the matter could now go for nothing, since evidently she was guilty of concealment in an important matter, and it might even be doubted whether she was not a party to the crime. The only alternative solution was that the can had been bought, borrowed or stolen by Tollard himself before the race started. In any case, the existence of a strange car no longer called for any credence. He determined to put the whole thing before Bredon the moment he could be got hold of. Nor had he long to wait ; Bredon appeared at the rendezvous within an hour of breakfast.

" It's all very well," objected Bredon, " but you haven't even the beginnings of a case against either of them. If you'd tied them up at the inquest with all these difficulties, at least the public mind might have associated them in some way with Worsley's death. But now you haven't even any status for asking them questions. And it doesn't work, you know. Assuming, as you do, that Tollard had finished off his man before midnight, the last thing he was likely to do was to hang about the road in the hope of somebody coming past. Obviously, he'd have driven hell-for-leather to King's Norton, told us that his breakdown hadn't been as bad as he'd feared, and trusted to the speed he'd made to give him a sort of an alibi."

187

" Yes, but I'm not so sure now that the death did happen before midnight. What if they were both in this thing, and it was necessary, somehow, for both to be on the spot before they could pull the murder off ? In that case, you see, it was rather ingenious for them to have two separate excuses, Tollard breaking down and Miss Morel getting herself held up by the police. Tollard waits at the side of the road till his accomplice drives back from Hereford and joins him. That appears to dissociate them altogether."

" Yes, but why didn't they tell the same story about their movements ? "

" Bluff, and rather ingenious at that. They foresaw that the Coroner would conclude exactly what he did conclude – that they came back to Lastbury at different times, not having met on the way, and that Miss Morel must have seen some other car and mistaken it for Tollard's."

" Well, even so you've got to get over the medico's evidence. By your new account of it, the murder must have been done about one o'clock in the morning. Whereas the medico thought it was before midnight."

" Still, he wasn't certain."

" And there's another thing ; if they came back at half-past twelve, why didn't they find Worsley asleep in bed ? "

" Oh, that was his business. We know that

188

he *was* sitting up, because he made a point of asking to be called later than usual the next morning. Of course, they took risks ; the servants might have been back by one o'clock – actually they weren't, quite. But I don't suppose they expected the servants to be away ; they probably waited till one so as to be certain nobody would be about."

" Well, what are you going to do about it ? Make an arrest and bluff them ? "

" Of course you know I can't do anything of the kind. No, the only thing I can do is to stay on here and watch them – him especially. Come to think of it, why is he still hanging round here ? Or she ? Surely it would be decent to go away, with the house more or less in mourning ? "

" So far as she's concerned, I gather she stays on because Mrs. Halliford wants her to ; she likes to have a woman about the house. With Tollard it's different ; indeed, I can't quite make out what he's up to. Mrs. Halliford told Angela last night she couldn't understand why he showed no signs of budging ; said he'd been here best part of three weeks, and young men have no manners nowadays. If you ask me, I think he's struck on Miss Morel and just can't tear himself away."

" There you are, you see ; you admit they're hand in glove."

" I don't admit anything of the kind. Angela, who pretends to have a kind of second sight about these things, assures me that Tollard is in love with Miss Morel, but that proves nothing. However, if you're going to keep an eye on Tollard, you'd better start in straight away. He told us at breakfast he was going into Hereford this morning, and asked us if he could do any commissions for us. I don't mind giving you that amount of stable information."

" Good man! I'll be going in too. It's a nuisance that I've nobody with me to shadow him; he knows me by sight, more's the pity. Still, I think I can keep beneath the skyline all right."

" How are you going to manage for a car? "

" Oh, I came in one; it's parked up at the pub in the village. I'll fetch it out now and lie up on the other side of the bridge. What make of car is his? Oh, good; one can recognise them easily."

Leyland had a principle that when you were out to shadow anybody, you should start in front of them and let them pass you. It prevented their suspecting you from the outset, and it gave you a tactical advantage in having one good look at them. He hung about in his own car close to the side of the road, just beyond the bridge, until he heard a hoot at the corner and saw, in his reflector, his quarry coming down the slope of the hill. Then he started himself, at a good round pace, so that he had gone several hundred yards before he waved to Tollard to pass. At the moment of passing, Tollard's attention was necessarily taken up with the road, while Leyland shot a look at him in which he discovered that he was alone, that he had no luggage, that he was not dressed as if for a train journey. This was not an escape, then ; but it was worth following the expedition up, to see what company this mysterious literary man kept, at Hereford or beyond it.

The first visit was to a garage ; and here Tollard broke the rules of the game by leaving his car, evidently with directions that it should be overhauled somehow. When you were in a car, and the man you were shadowing was on foot, it was always difficult to say whether you did better to alight yourself or not. But in the streets of a town a car suffers from too many handicaps. Leyland waited till he came to a convenient inn and parked his own car there, waiting in the shadow of the arch until his man came past. He followed at a good distance ; they were evidently making for the middle of the town, and it would be time to close in when the pavements grew more crowded. Tollard's objective, it proved, was a rather improbable one ; he turned into the cathedral. Churches, in these materialistic days, no longer afford sanctuary for the fugitive, but there are some of them which are uncommonly useful, for all that, to the criminal classes – they have doors opening on different streets, and sometimes, in the darkness of the aisles, you can dodge your pursuer.

A cathedral close, though, is not often much use unless you are on calling terms with the canons. Leyland assumed that Tollard was merely sight-seeing, and that he would not appear till ten minutes or more were up ; he hastened, therefore, to secure an ally from the local police-station, in case there should be need of watching some building by two entrances at once. They stood together looking into a shop window, uninteresting indeed (for it was a milliner's) but convenient because it had a large looking-glass at the side which enabled them to watch the entrance to the close. Twenty minutes they waited, twenty-five minutes, and then Tollard came out, not with any relish of salvation in his demeanour, but carefree evidently. He looked up at a clock, which said twenty minutes to twelve ; verified the time on his own watch, and then dived into a hairdresser's. He seemed unconsciously determined to make the task of the watchers as wearisome as possible. Leyland had no idea one could get so tired of a busy street as he did of that excellent main thoroughfare which runs through Hereford.

Droves of cattle went past ; a lorry which appeared to contain about half an aeroplane ; a steam-roller, and a small procession of sand-wichmen in white smocks and white hats, advertising somebody's cider. But all these excitements, which aroused a good deal of comment among the professional street loungers, failed to excite you when you were keeping one eye open all the time on the entrance to a barber's shop, and were not certain whether the man inside would, or would not, have a shampoo.

A minute or two after twelve he reappeared, duly shorn ; and now a consultation of his watch seemed to warn him, as it had warned Leyland yesterday, that a thoughtful Government was alive to the fact of human thirst. He had a look at one or two places of entertainment and finished up at an unpretentious public house, of the repellent type that is faced with encaustic tiles. It was doing business, however, this thirsty morning ; a glance at the passage showed you that the sandwichmen had already seized the opportunity of easing their shoulders here. Leyland wondered if it would be politic to send his assistant in to join the company, but decided to reserve him for more serious needs. The sandwichmen, evidently, had not yet reached their luncheon-hour, for they came out again in ten minutes or so and passed back down the street ; a blurred outline behind the frosted glass showed that the bar was still tenanted by a solitary figure.

Dreary as the previous watches had been, this one proved a purgatory. One o'clock struck, and hooters went off, and bank doors were locked, and people started going home from offices, and the sandwichmen, now prepared to call it a day, made haste to put the frosted glass between themselves and the staring eyes of the world once more. Then at last Tollard came out ; you almost wondered to find him unaffected by his interminable potations. Now at least, if he was engaged on any significant errand, his movements should betray him. There was a sickening fear in Leyland's heart as they passed the cathedral again – yes, back by the same street by which they had come, there was really no doubt of it. It was as a mere formality that he sent his assistant on ahead while he retrieved his own car from its garage ; and it was with no hope of further incident that he followed, doggedly, at a distance, till the car in front of him turned the corner into Lastbury. He had spent the morning playing with shadows.

CHAPTER XX : A SUNDAY MORNING PUZZLE

THERE IS AN hour, just before luncheon on Sunday, when time seems to stand still. It is our inheritance from the days when people used to go to church ; you came out ravenous from the effects of the sermon and found that, since the servants had been worshipping too, there was no chance of getting any food served for an hour yet. In London, you filled in the interval by walking about in the park bowing to your friends ; in the country, by going round the farm. In my own youth, believe it or not, we used to sit down and write out an abstract of the sermon ; an admirable principle, since it not only kept us quiet during those harrowing minutes, but taught us, thus early, to practise the art (now unhappily lost by journalism) of reporting from memory. In these days, when most people do not go to church, the same affliction befalls us ; with the best will in the world (unless you are a puzzle-solver) you cannot make the Sunday papers last out beyond noon ; and at noon, though you are ready for the midday meal, you cannot ask the servants to produce it ; that would look as if they had not been to church either. It is at this moment that, if Governments were more enlightened, we should turn our clocks on for summer-time.

Such was the hour when Miles Bredon sat in the library at Lastbury, torturing himself with one of those ingenious crosswords which are supplied to the *Onlooker* by the anonymous gentleman who signs himself " Topcliffe." The library was not really a library ; there were no grim lines of Victorian pulpit oratory, no bound *Punches*, no eighteenth century travels, no County histories, no collections of old ballads – nothing that the word " library " should con-note. But there was a silting-up, in this room, of stodgy volumes given as Christmas presents, of technical manuals about agriculture, in a word, of all the books that were not being read and not likely to be read ; the Hallifords, therefore, had furnished it with a profusion of badly stamped notepaper and unnecessary sealing-wax, and the room contained neither loud speaker nor gramophone. It was the refuge of the studiously inclined ; and, as we have seen, it was here that Worsley was last known to have had speech with his fellow-men. This Sunday morning, it was more tenanted than usual ; Halliford was there, beguiling his

Sunday rest with a monograph on fish-manures, and his wife, deserting her sanctum for once, was writing letters at a side table.

Halliford picked from between the pages of his book a folded slip of paper, unnoticed until his reading brought him to it. " This yours, Myrtle ? " he asked, when he had knitted his brows over it for a little. " All Greek to me ; shorthand or something." His wife came and bent over him, one knee on the arm of his chair. " Looks more like cipher," she corrected. " Those marks wouldn't be easy enough to make, would they, for shorthand. Mr. Bredon will be able to tell us ; here's a puzzle for you, Mr. Bredon, much more instructive than Topcliffe, I expect." And she brought it over to him as he looked up blinking from his remote world of Down and Across.

" You might call it either," he admitted. " It's one of those early shorthands ; I used to go in for the thing rather at one time – Mason's, I think, but I'm not sure. They weren't phonetic, of course ; just represented the ordinary written letters of the alphabet by symbols. Yes, it's Mason or an adaptation of him. I can't remember the system precisely, but I can work it out soon enough on the ordinary deciphering principles. Leave me alone with it for a minute or two, and I'll report."

His diagnosis was correct, and before long he

had transcribed into longhand this much of his original : " Dined at the M's to meet Sandwood, one of the fifteen or sixteen young men at present in the House who think they are destined to be dictator. He seems to bring no qualifications to the task except the conviction that his ancestors, including the present peer, have been Die-hards ; his inclination is certainly rather to live easy. His platform is merely one of State Socialism, which differs from that of the present administration only in being more vocal." There could be no doubt at all about this ; it was an extract – a page, now he came to examine the paper more closely – from a private diary, kept in shorthand. Only one man ever came to Lastbury who moved in the world, or was capable of the criticisms, which the document exhibited. Bredon was still holding it at arm's length, wondering whether any concealment about it was either possible or desirable, when Mrs. Halliford bore down on him. " Well, Mr. Bredon, what is it ? Buried treasure, or somebody's marriage lines, or what ? " The seriousness of his face checked her. " Not – not something of Cecil's ? " " Yes, I don't think there can be any doubt of that. He must have picked up that book, while he was going round the shelves in here, and used that sheet as a book-mark. It's a bit of his diary ; a page which has come loose.

You can see the gum on the edges ; a lazy binder has cut one separate page and gummed it in. Such pages always come loose, and this one has. I haven't got the date ; but I dare say we shall be able to guess about that when I have worked on a little further. Here it is, as far as it's got." And he showed her the extract.

Mrs. Halliford read it slowly, half turning so as to share it with her husband, who had come up and stood beside her. "Yes," she said, "that's Cecil all right. I remember his saying something of the kind about young Sandwood when he was last here ; let's see, when would that be, Walter ? April, wouldn't it ? But that's too poignant – to be eavesdropping in Cecil's private diary now."

"We ought to send it to the executors," Halliford pointed out, in a more practical spirit. "Odd, now, I never knew he kept a diary."

"Oh, but of course he did ! Don't you remember once when he read us his impressions of Poland out of it ? And he must have brought it here with him, because he was very faithful about keeping it up to date. He always wrote it up before he went to bed at night."

"I suppose," hazarded Bredon, "the book itself wouldn't be about here too ? "

"It's hardly likely. You see, a whole lot of papers and things were left, a few in here and the rest in his bedroom. I told the servants to pack them all up, just as they were, and send them to the executors; I couldn't bear to finger them myself, just then. I'll certainly send this page on to-night; they may be wanting to publish some of it, of course. It looks rather intimate, though. Do go on a bit, Mr. Bredon; we aren't likely to come across anything we oughtn't to see. And indeed, I think Cecil would as soon we read his diary as anybody. How clever of you to be able to read it so fast. May I watch you doing it? "

Miles Bredon was not a vain man; but even the most modest of the human race have their own pet accomplishments, which a very little encouragement will induce them to parade. His was a mind which delighted in mystifications, and he had made a study of early short-hands and ciphers, partly because it was sometimes useful to him in the way of business, partly because it appealed to him. It is to be feared that he came near to falling into the manner of a lecturer, little as he loved his present audience. Mrs. Halliford listened to him with every appearance of deep attention, but her husband, who knew her better, strongly suspected that she was already repenting the interest she had shown in a technical subject which really bored her. And indeed she was scarcely an apt pupil; pointing now and again to a particular symbol with " That's an F, isn't it ? " or " Here comes R again," and nearly always getting it wrong.

There would be no point in printing the whole of the document as Bredon deciphered it. It must suffice to say that, from internal evidence, they concluded it must be a page belonging to late March or early April of the current year. Worsley, it seemed, must have put it between the pages of a book he had picked up casually – " of course, he was interested in *everything*," Mrs. Halliford explained – merely to preserve it from loss ; nothing in the entry suggested that it was of special importance or that it had been torn out in repentance over some too harshly worded phrase. It was incredibly neat, like everything Worsley did ; the lines being spaced so exactly that you might have taken it for printing.

" Now, why would a feller do that ? " asked Halliford at luncheon. " Would the idea be that it was less trouble to write that way, or that you got more into a small space, or that if the ordinary person came across it they couldn't read it ? "

" All three, I imagine," said Bredon, " but the last chiefly. Not, of course, that you'd expect a document written like that to defy all efforts at deciphering it. Very doubtful, I should think, whether it would be possible to turn out a lot of stuff like that without giving away your code to the trained eye, however secret it was. But your ordinary housemaid, who has no scruple whatever about private documents, is not going to be bothered with decoding cryptograms. Ordinary Pitman shorthand would be easier to write, naturally ; but that would mean that any well-trained secretary or reporter could read it at a glance, and a public man, writing frankly like that, wouldn't want to run the risk of either. So he taught himself an old-fashioned cipher instead."

Halliford was gazing out of the window, evidently in two minds whether to speak or be silent. Then he turned to his wife and said, " You know, Myrtle, I wish we'd kept that diary and got Mr. Bredon to decode some of it for us. Perhaps we could get the executors to let us have a look at it – the last part, I mean."

" What on earth for ? "

" Oh, well, don't you see, in a diary like that he's bound to have put down something about how he was feeling, whether he was in good spirits or not, and all that. Or, even if he didn't put it down on purpose, one could read between the lines. And I think we'd be able to make a better guess whether it was really an accident, or whether – whether he'd driven himself almost mad with overwork and took the short way out of it. That's all I meant."

" Yes, if you feel you need that. Personally, I've never had any doubts. But I should think the trustees would let us have a look ; when I write to them I'll suggest it. I only hope it hasn't miscarried."

THE HOUSE-PARTY at Lastbury, it need hardly
be said, had shrunk considerably by now. The
Arnolds, since they lived near by, had left on
the very day of the tragedy ; the Carberrys
had waited only for the inquest. Nobody
remained except the guests who stayed on by
the express wish of their hostess, and Tollard,
who seemed insensible to the decencies of the
situation. Mrs. Halliford still exclaimed, occasionally, what a comfort Bredon's presence
was to her husband, but the position was not
without its difficulties. For one thing, it is not
very easy to be always forcing yourself on
your host's company. And there was a worse
uneasiness lurking in his mind which he ex-
pounded to Angela on the Sunday evening.
The other four were playing bridge, to tide
over the necessary interval between tea and
dinner, with incidental music from some foreign
broadcasting station. It seemed a better way
of passing the time to sit on the river's very
edge, fresh from bathing, and listen to the
distant tinkle of church bells higher up the

valley, the plop of rising salmon and the lapping of the water round the stern of a moored punt.

"It's not that I don't like Halliford," said Bredon; "I do rather, and I'm considerably sorry for him. And it's not that I regard myself as being on in this show; they may say what they will, but as long as I am not working for the company I *will* not go round playing the detective; I will notice nothing except what is thrust under my nose. But I have the uneasy feeling that if I were taking any sort of hand in this job, I wouldn't be going round fraternising with Halliford so much. I would be sitting down in a cool hour, with a wet towel round my head, asking myself exactly what Halliford was doing between a quarter and half past ten on Tuesday night."

Angela unclasped her hands from her knees and turned towards him, sucking a stalk of grass. "I thought we'd agreed to rule that idea out altogether, seeing that the Hallifords were both fond of Worsley and stood to lose any amount by his death. In fact, I suppose they have lost it. Where's the sense?"

"I know. It's absurd to think one can leave motive out of account. But I have a suspicion, sometimes, that I'm really using this motive business as an excuse for burying my head in the sand. Do you mind if I tell you, just to get it off my chest, what I *should*

205

be thinking if it were possible to imagine the Hallifords wanting Worsley out of the way ? "

" All right, release it ; it can't do any harm. But remember that Myrtle Halliford is a particular friend of mine, won't you ? "

" Blast her. What was I going to say ? Yes, look at this first ; I simply can't imagine why Leyland hasn't thought of it. Though it's true it only occurred to me quite lately. Don't you see that the murder, if it was one, was almost certainly committed by somebody who knew, beforehand, that Worsley was going to be left behind at Lastbury that night ; that he wouldn't be careering about in a car all over Worcestershire ? "

" Oo, yes, that's rather a point. Certainly it's a point. As for instance Mr. Tollard, not being the eloping female himself, was in no position to know who the eloping male was, and that it wasn't Worsley ? "

" Exactly. How you see things ! Halliford, on the other hand, *did* know who was the eloping male, so he did know that Worsley would be left at home and wouldn't be missed, if he disappeared, till the next morning. Now, let's indulge this fancy. If Halliford did it, when did he do it ? "

" Not before 10.10, because the footman saw Worsley then. Indeed, not before 10.20, because Halliford was with us in the drawing-room

206

till about then. But from then till 10.40——"

" From 10.20 till 10.40 he was under no observation at all. And during that time we know that he was supposed to be going down to the drive gate, which is almost next door to the silo. What's to prevent him looking in at Worsley's room on the way, and getting him to come for a stroll ? "

" The library, you mean ? Or Worsley's bedroom ? "

" Confound the woman, now she's taken to asking awkward questions. As you say, if Worsley was already beginning to undress, wouldn't the suggestion of a stroll seem rather untimely ? Whereas, if he was still in the library, why did he park that curious assort-ment of his belongings in the bedroom before the stroll came off ? That needs thinking of ; we will consider it later on. At present, we assume the stroll. By what way did they go, the drive gate ? "

" By the path through the walled garden, you want me to say. Because that is where the cap was left, and the white favour, and the cigar-end."

" Don't hang on to that cigar-end too much ; it may have been an accident. I can't remember whether Halliford was smoking in the drawing-room, can you ? No, I thought not. But the cap, as you say, and the favour want some

207

explaining. They would be explained if Halliford walked down that path with Worsley –
who knows ? – beside him, on the roundabout
way to the front gate."

" Wouldn't he be rather careful not to shed
little mementoes like that ?   Oo !   Did you see
that salmon ? "

" Attend, woman.   A paper cap slips from
your head very easily without your noticing it
the favour probably wants a different explanation, which we'll come to later on.   He drops
the cap, anyhow, from carelessness.   They reach
the silo ;   what do they do ? "

" Climb up to have a look at the moon."

" Shut up ;   there wouldn't be time, anyway.
No, they get into the silo to have one last look
for that pipe, so essential, Halliford says, to
him before the expedition starts.   Of course
Worsley offers to help.   While he is searching,
Halliford gets out, and, standing there on the
stanchions, begins quietly shutting the hatches.
Worsley does not understand what is happening until it is too late ;   he is a prisoner."

" What was the pitchfork for, by the way ? "
It was understood that, in an interview like
the present, it was Angela's job to take on the
part of the *advocatus diaboli* and make all the
objections that occurred to her, whether she
thought them important or not.

" I don't think it was *for* anything.   I think

Halliford tidied it away, some time before dinner, by putting it in the silo. Assuming all this nonsense I'm talking to be the truth, of course he wouldn't leave it there when he was going to shut Worsley in. You can use a pitch-fork in all sorts of ways, as a battering-ram, for example. But a man without a weapon, shut in by those hatches which afford you no handhold to climb up by, and cannot be opened from the inside, is your prisoner as long as he is weaponless. Also he is in a lethal chamber, so that by morning he will be found dead."

" And how long a time interval are you allowing for all that ? Mrs. Halliford was rootling round in the car by half-past ten or soon after, just close to the silo. Wouldn't she be rather surprised about it all ? "

" Yes, she'd be surprised, unless——"

" Now, Miles, remember she's a friend of mine ! No, but it would be too fantastic to suppose they were both in it ; the motive would become more complicated than ever. I think you'd better make the whole thing take ten minutes or so."

" And why shouldn't it ? Assuming he can get Worsley to go with him in the first instance, it doesn't take long to reach the silo ; it doesn't take long for Halliford to persuade Worsley to come in and look round, and it doesn't take long to shut those doors. You'd only need to shut

209

about three, at the bottom, to make it impossible for the fellow inside to climb out. Then, perhaps as soon as he's finished, he sees the lights of the Mossman coming down the drive. He dodges behind the silo, I imagine ; and that's why he doesn't answer when she calls – it would be too difficult to explain why he was fooling round there. Also, he would like her to think he was somewhere else, just at the moment of the murder. So he holds his tongue ; Worsley, in the silo, doubtless doesn't ; but you don't get much chance of making your voice heard when you're shouting in a long tube like that. Halliford waits till she goes back ; then he nips round by the river path and makes for his room. There he is, all present and correct, by 10.40."

" Mmm, yes. Do you know, Miles, I don't believe this is one of your best efforts. I mean, the whole time-scheme is so dashed short. What if Worsley had said, " Just wait till I finish this paragraph," and taken five minutes over it ? What if he'd been in his bedroom, half undressed ? A murderer could hardly afford to take risks like that."

" I shouldn't wonder if you're right ; as I say, I don't really believe in all this, because of the want of motive. But let me finish ; the only way to get unreal doubts off your mind is to indulge them and see where they lead to.

When Halliford and his wife come back from King's Norton, he tells her to put the Mossman to bed, while he goes off into the drive to get the Bridge, which has been left standing there. That's in the evidence, and of course it looks as if he wanted to get her out of the way while he went and opened the hatches of the silo again. Actually, it seems, there was some difficulty about starting the Mossman ; so he must have nipped round through the walled garden, opened the hatches after she'd left and hared back down the drive so as to be in ahead of her."

" That just works, yes."

" Next morning, he obviously thinks he has got away with it and left no traces. Otherwise, he'd have cleared away that paper cap, for example, before he ever had me called. But he must have noticed it later and wondered, since he'd seen me going into the walled garden, whether I had noticed it too. If so, he thought, I shouldn't have known whose it was ; therefore he clears it away, as any gardener might have done, and puts down there instead Worsley's white favour, which had dropped . . . oh, anywhere. To make people think it was Worsley who dropped the cap, at the same time as he dropped the favour."

" A little elaborate, but let that pass."

" That business in the walled garden has *got*

211

to be elaborate, whatever you make of it. The thermometer, for example – why did Halliford want to set it, at a moment when he had no time to lose, just before the murder? And if it wasn't he who set it, or if he set it at some other time, earlier in the day, why did he want to pretend next morning, that it had never been set at all? No, it's elaborate all right."

" You don't think it could be a frame-up against Halliford – the murderer, or some accomplice, trying to make it look as if Halliford had done it?"

" No, the notion of a frame-up won't work. Because evidently the murderer wanted it to look as if it had been suicide or accident. He would be a fool if he went and spoiled that impression – God knows how cleverly produced – by leaving fake clues about to suggest that it *was* a murder after all. You can't have it both ways. Let's see, there was something we said we'd leave over till the end, wasn't there? Something that didn't quite fit in? "

" Yes ; about whether Worsley was in his bedroom or still in the library when Halliford asked him to come and take the air. Or rather, as it proved, the carbon dioxide."

" Must have been in his bedroom. There couldn't be any sense, otherwise, in his leaving that jumble of personal effects lying about. I suppose Halliford will have vamped up some

212

excuse of wanting to see him particularly, on business that wouldn't wait till the race was over. But, as you say, it doesn't work ; even if you leave motive out of account it doesn't really work. You're trying to open the door all the time with a key which doesn't fit. Well, fortunately there's no need to worry ; let us congratulate ourselves that it is no business of ours. And let us cheer up our depressed host as best we may. After all, he's not that kind of man, is he, when all's said and done. Hullo, are you going in again ? "

" Of course I am. The best bathe in the day is always the last. Do you know, Phyllis Morel said she didn't think Halliford was a murdering man ; or if he did commit a murder, she said, it would be a very straightforward one, because he'd think of it as if it were just killing a dog that had been worrying sheep. That's not this kind of murder, anyhow."

" You bet it isn't. If it is murder at all it's a mean one, quite certainly ; one that will make us disgusted with human nature, if we weren't already."

NEXT DAY THE numbers of the party were to be still further reduced. Tollard had given intimation overnight to a barely protesting hostess that he must make a move soon after breakfast ; and at breakfast itself Phyllis Morel received a letter which made her presence in London necessary, she said, that evening. Luncheon she could wait for, but it must be no longer. Mrs. Halliford, also, had news by the morning's post.

" This is too extraordinary," she said, " after what we were talking about yesterday. Here's a letter from the executors to say that poor Cecil's diary was not returned among his other things. Knowing his methodical habits, they say, they think it is probable the book must be here still. We must have a hunt in the library afterwards, Walter."

It was Bredon himself who actually made the discovery. The diary had been thrust into one of the shelves, doubtless by some over-tidy housemaid, next to a set of books whose bindings it remotely resembled. Who does not know the housemaid's capacity for finding the most improbable resemblances between books ? They found, without difficulty, the place where the gummed sheet had come loose, and there was no doubt about its fitting exactly into the context. But they were not yet, it seemed, at the end of their mystery. The writing in the diary finished off at the bottom of a page, and the next two pages had been neatly torn out – not with any attempt at disguise, but so as to leave a narrow margin of paper close to the sewed edge.

" How far down does it go ? " asked Angela.

" No doubt about that," said her husband, as he scrutinised the crabbed symbols. " Here is the date fully given. He wrote up his diary on that last night ; but it ends in the middle of a sentence and at the bottom of a page. It looks as if he had either stopped short, and then torn out two pages ; or, more probably of course, as if he had finished his sentence, but the page on which he finished it was torn out since."

" Why, I wonder ? " asked Halliford.

" Any amount of possible reasons," explained Bredon cheerfully. " He wrote something which he afterwards wanted to withdraw ; tidier really to cut the page or pages out than to black out the passage, and safer. Or there may have been just a line or two of script which he didn't notice, and he tore out what he thought were two blank pages for some delicate piece of writing ; it's good paper, you see. I suppose there's no chance of the missing sheets being somewhere lying about, Mrs. Halliford ? The wastepaper basket will have been cleared long ago. Is there a dustbin we could try ? "

" I think they keep papers undestroyed for a week or so," said Mrs. Halliford vaguely. " An idea of Riddell's, in case anything should be missing. I'll show him the size of page and ask him to have a look. Meanwhile, we've got to see Adrian Tollard off. Thank you so much, Mr. Bredon ; you're winning all the honours."

They assembled at the front door – all the party except Phyllis Morel, who was not to be found. Tollard had just driven his car round from the garage. His farewells were conventional and brief ; he seemed to be in a great hurry and flung his suit-case down beside him, instead of opening the capacious dicky of his two-seater. He had only just disappeared when Bredon was called to the telephone.

" Leyland speaking ; from the village. Has Tollard gone yet ? Damn ; I must follow him. I say, can you lend me your car ? Mine won't start, God knows why. Thanks awfully ; you couldn't drive it out now and meet me just outside the gate ? . . . Who ? Oh, Mrs. Bredon ; yes, of course she'll do ; rather. I'll explain when I come back."

Angela made no difficulty about her mission ; and fortunately she had not to look far for an excuse. Tollard had managed to leave a fishing-rod behind in his hurry ; and as it was known that he would be delayed in Hereford on business, she volunteered to catch him up and deliver it to him. Her husband refused to come with her ; " It'd only make the car heavier," he said, " and I've got to do a little more decipher-ing to satisfy Mrs. Halliford's curiosity – not to mention my own." With the instinct we all have for keeping the interesting part to the last, he began deciphering, not at the very end but at the point where the entry for Worsley's last day began. There was no suggestion at all here that Worsley had anything on his mind, or that he experienced the symptoms of any nervous complaint. There was a careful des-cription of the way in which the salmon didn't rise ; some mild complaints about the ubiquity of gramophones at Lastbury ; extracts from an agricultural conversation with Arnold ; some other references to the company, among which Bredon blushed to find himself described as a likeable fellow ; fears about the progress of the article ; an analysis of the afternoon's post . . .

He was still transcribing this, somewhat wearily, when the butler came in. " Mrs. Halliford's compliments, sir, and would this be the piece of paper you were requiring ? " A

217

glance left no doubt of that ; but there was only one piece. Bredon took it and gave a sigh of relief : it had writing on it.

" You're sure there was no other like this ? " he asked the butler.

" No, sir ; the girls looked very carefully through the whole pile. Nothing at all of a similar character, sir."

That was odd. Whatever happened, you would expect to find that neither piece had disappeared or both. The salvaged piece had only a single line of writing on it, at the top of the page. Was this the direct continuation of what Worsley had been writing, and was the lost sheet blank ? Or had the lost sheet been fully covered with writing, and was this a mere colophon ? That could be seen, presumably, as soon as the decoding was finished ; it would not be long now. Five minutes later, he had completed the deciphering of the book, whose last sentence was unfinished : *I have put down my entry early to-night, because I am to . . .* The single sentence on the torn-off sheet ran, *. . . be blamed already for not obeying my doctor, who says I should always go to bed at eleven.*

Yes, that looked all right. That would mean that the lost sheet was a mere blank ; odd that it should happen that way. He looked at the reverse side of the sheet in his hand and found it disfigured by an enormous blot, such as is produced by a sudden hæmorrhage in one's fountain pen. It had evidently dried of itself while the book was still closed ; the pages had stuck together, and when they were pulled apart they had been pulled apart unskilfully, so that a thin film of paper from the opposite page had been left clinging to the surface of the ink. Come, that made things more intelligible. A man like Worsley would hate to have a blot intruding on his diary ; he would cut out both pages when he discovered what had happened ; and then – perhaps he never noticed that this meant sacrificing a line of his manuscript ; perhaps he noticed, and meant to make good the omission later on. Another sign, perhaps, of that unexpected interruption of Worsley's plans which there had already been reason to postulate.

Almost mechanically, though, Bredon held up the paper to the light. It was good paper, and (unlike most diary paper) had a watermark. This promised to be interesting ; it was worth making sure that there was a watermark – and the same watermark – in the leaves which still remained in the book. Yes, here it was, the maker's name ; and, from some trick in the cutting, it did not appear uniformly on the page ; now it would come higher up, now lower down. So there was a further test to be

219

applied ; did the sheet he held in his hand fit on to the thin remnant of paper opposite the last entry in the diary ? He made the experiment with little hope of a significant result ; then he gave a long drawn whistle. It was no fit at all ; the edges of the watermark did not nearly meet. His second experiment he felt to be a foregone conclusion. Apply the cut-off sheet to the edge where the second page had been torn out, and the fit was perfect. It was the first sheet, presumably containing the immediate continuation of the diary, which was missing after all.

He went to the window, and stood for a while staring out of it. Yes, of course it was just conceivably possible that the words *be blamed already* only fitted on to the words *I am to* by an odd coincidence, though it was not only the words which fitted, it was the whole context. Just conceivably possible, therefore, that there *was* a whole page of manuscript missing, instead of a blank page as he had supposed. But that, even apart from the coincidence, landed you in difficulties. As long as you assumed that the salvaged sheet was the first of the two, then the blot explained itself ; the other side of the blot would be on the lost page. But if the salvaged sheet was the second, not the first, then the blot on the back of it should have blotted onto the first blank page left in the book – and there was no mark. Bredon hesitated a little ; then, with the air of a man whose mind is made up, he carried the book and the loose sheet up to Mrs. Halliford's boudoir. He found it empty. Ten minutes later he was going upstairs, three steps at a time, to his bedroom. From the back of a drawer he took out one, two, three, four packs of patience cards and began playing the great game whose rules only he understood. When his wife returned, it was to find the whole floor of the bedroom littered with pasteboard and Bredon, on all fours, making his way gingerly from row to row.

It is time, perhaps, that we followed her in her rival adventures. Leyland was waiting for her immediately outside the drive gate and sprang in before she had time to pull up completely. " It's nice to be on the warpath again," she said. " But what is biting you, exactly, over this expedition of Mr. Tollard's ? It was only the day before yesterday you were making a criminal of him because he would go on staying at Lastbury. Now you're making a criminal of him because he's leaving it. Why exactly ? "

" It's not the fact of his leaving so much as the circumstances. I suppose you know Miss Morel is in the dicky ? "

" Phyllis Morel ? She wasn't when he started."

" Excuse me, but did you open it to see ? "

" But . . . you don't mean . . . he hasn't . . ."

" Oh, she walked in of her own accord, if that's what you mean. And I imagine he let her out as soon as they got out of sight. But it struck me as a rather noticeable circumstance, and I ran back at top speed to the local inn to get my car. She was out of order, wouldn't budge. Now, I know she was all right yesterday ; and it looks to me very much as if my friend Mr. Tollard had not been anxious to have any followers. Which is why I'm determined to follow him."

" What on earth are they up to ? And, for that matter, where on earth are we going ? Hereford is a fairly safe assumption, but we haven't the remotest chance of overhauling them before they get there. What do we do next ? "

" Lord knows. We'll try the first policeman on point duty ; with luck he might have noticed them. Otherwise I can think of no hope, except of course the people who lounge about in the Square ; they're apt to notice things."

But the loungers were never questioned. The very first policeman applied to beamed all over with intelligence ; " Yes," he said, " they left a message for you : said you was to go straight to the Green Dragon and wait ; they wouldn't be above ten minutes or so."

" Man alive, what's the good of that to us ? " expostulated Leyland. " Which road did they take ? "

" Well, I can't say as I noticed that particularly. They put the car up in the Green Dragon, you see, and then came across to talk to me. I shouldn't think they was far off, but which street I couldn't say."

Angela was lying back against the cushions of the car, shouting with laughter. She had never seriously believed that they were on the track of a criminal ; but this gloriously tame end to their expedition took her altogether by surprise. She led the half convinced Leyland to the rendezvous and tried to get him interested in the motoring papers which were its only available literature. Punctually to their time, the two missing members of the house-party arrived and made straight for them. " I say," explained Tollard awkwardly, " I'm afraid I've been leading you rather a dance, but I swear it was with the best intentions. Oh, I forget you hadn't been introduced – this is the gentleman I've told you so much about – this is Mrs. Tollard."

" I HATE TO seem inquisitive," pleaded Angela,
when the first shock of gasping and congratula-
tion was over, " but could we have some idea
of what it was all about ? "

" Certainly you shall," said Phyllis. " I've
got to keep on the right side of you, because
later on, when we've had cocktails, I am going
to cadge a ride off you, back to Lastbury in
time for lunch. I've got my things to pack
still. You tell them, Adrian. I've been making
so many improbable statements this morning
that I'm quite hoarse with it."

" It all seems so silly when you explain it,"
objected Tollard. " Anyhow, it started with
an argument we had the day after the eloping
race. I said the whole idea of eloping seemed
tiresomely old-fashioned nowadays, when the
law was so obliging about waiving all impedi-
ments, except youth and tea-time. And I said
that two people who happened to be staying at
the same house could easily go off and get
married before the rest of the party knew what

224

they were up to. Then we had a bet on it, and in order to try out the bet we decided to make the experiment ourselves. Then the question arose whether we should just *pretend* to get married, or really get married so as to make the whole thing more realistic. Phyllis seemed to think——"

" You hound ! "

" Oh, well, have it your own way ; we settled that we might as well do it really ; so we have. Phyllis, of course, was on her honour to back me up as best she could. You see, we're both rather mad on treasure hunts and all that sort of idea, so it seemed as if a wedding would be more fun if we dispensed with the bridesmaids and the cake and all that and turned it into a sort of marriage by capture. The only bother was that I was perfectly right ; we had no difficulty at all in keeping the thing absolutely secret ; there could be no eloping race because there would be nobody in pursuit. That's where you came in so handy, sir."

" Oh," said Leyland, with a grimace, " you've been using me as a sort of property policeman, have you ? "

" I'm afraid that's about the size of it. You see, somehow or another I felt certain you were a cop when I saw you at the inquest. That sounds a frightfully rude thing to say ; because of course I suppose you were trying to look as if you weren't one. But when I was making

225

my statement I looked round the court, and I felt all the time, *That's the man who's out for my blood*. Just afterwards, if you remember, I came up and talked to you ; and then my suspicions were confirmed. I don't know if you ever really fish, but you weren't fishing then – not in the river, I mean. You were fishing for incriminating remarks from me all right. Well, I knew it must all look pretty thick about the time I got back to Lastbury that night, so I wasn't surprised. But I thought I would take you on, and by Jove I did. I could have cried with enjoyment when I saw you waiting for me and shadowing me, that day I went down into Hereford to get the licence."

" I must begin to think about retiring. I'm losing my technique. All the same, I held you up that time."

" Well, yes, in a way. I could see it would be easier to dodge you on foot, that's why I parked the car and went to have a look at the cathedral."

" You didn't hope to get a marriage licence from the verger ? "

" No, but he jolly well told me where the bargain basement was. Then I just went up into the tower, and had a good look at you and your friend, so that I'd be sure of knowing you again."

" I could forgive you that, but not the wait while you were at the barber's."

" I went there because I wanted to think the thing out a bit. Nothing like a shampoo for clearing one's brains. I hadn't any real plan, though, till I saw those sandwichmen going into the pub."

" You don't mean you——"

" Yes, I had to. I wanted that licence, you see, and it wouldn't do to let you see where I was going, because you would tell your friends up at Lastbury about it, and I should lose my bet. *Anyone in the house* – that was laid down in the conditions. So I hired the coat and hat and the rest of the outfit for half a crack from one of the artists, and by Jove I walked out right under your nose. I parked the properties in a side alley, went and got my licence, with very little trouble, and came back to the bar, joining up again in the procession. So there I was all right."

Leyland's admiration of this saga was plainly fighting with his distrust of the man, which was still undispelled. " You know, Mr. Tollard," put in Angela, " Mr. Leyland is really dying to ask you about what happened on the night of the murder. I suppose I'm saying the wrong thing ; but wouldn't it be simplest if you told us something about that ? "

" Well, really, Mrs. Bredon," began Leyland uncomfortably.

" I know what you're going to say," suggested

227

Tollard; "you're going to say that if I make any statement you'll have to take notes of it, and they may be used against me afterwards. I'm prepared to risk that; I can't clear myself, unfortunately, but at least I can tell my story. The only bother is, it makes me hot all over to think of it even now. Phyllis, I think it had better be your turn, if you don't mind."

"All right; I've nothing to be ashamed of. First of all, let me explain why Adrian fell out of the race. You don't believe it, of course, but it was an honest-to-God breakdown. I've handled a good few, and I know when a car can't be made to go. It was water in the petrol tank all right; though the fool hadn't had the common sense to diagnose that and had wasted no end of time treating her for other ailments."

"Excuse me, Miss Morel, but have you any idea how the water got there? I mean, could that have happened by a mere accident?"

"Could have, theoretically. There are such things as faulty tins, though I'd raise pretty good hell if one of them got into my garage. No, it might just have been an accident, but it looked a long sight more as if somebody had been trying to nobble the favourite. It's a very easy way, you see, to engineer a breakdown, putting a cupful of water in the tank. And that, of course, was how all the trouble started."

228

"The engine trouble, you mean," asked Angela, "or——"

"No ; heart trouble. Adrian, I don't know if you've ever noticed it, is a mass of vanity. Having had his car specially overhauled before the race started, he was no end puzzled when she wouldn't go, and he leapt to the conclusion that somebody had been playing games. There wasn't the least likelihood of Myrtle Halliford's having done it, because that car of Adrian's wasn't due to make King's Norton till about cockcrow. So, my dear, what do you think he imagined ? He actually imagined that *I* had doped his car, and then had deliberately got myself into trouble with the police, so that we could both fall out of the race and have a jolly evening at Lastbury together. Tell me, are all men like that ? "

"Well, you must admit it looked jolly fishy," complained Tollard shamefacedly. "After all, you were the big authority on cars."

"Thinking it, even, was bad enough ; but when it comes to *saying* it. . . . Do you know that when I slowed down on the road to see if I could help him, all he said was, *Oh, so you've come back* ? "

"There wasn't any *so*. I just said *Oh, you've come back* – meaning nothing by it."

"I knew what you meant all right. And of course we had a first class row there and then.

I told him all sorts of things about himself. I pumped out his tank for him and gave him a fill of petrol ; but I said I wouldn't be seen going home with him ; he was to wait ten minutes and then follow. So we parted brass rags."

" Excuse me," interrupted Leyland. " What time was this ? "

" About a quarter past twelve, really. I had to make it later in my evidence, so as to pretend that I didn't stop. We must have been ten minutes or a quarter of an hour getting the car right, or rather, me showing him how to do it. Then I got home at the time I said, a little before the half hour ; he ran in about a quarter of an hour later. We'd agreed on the story we were going to tell, which was that I passed him without stopping, and he got petrol from another car. I didn't want it to be known I'd even been seen talking to him. And I stuck to that story all right, next day. But he went and invented a new story of his own, so as to pretend he was the first to get in. He thought, apparently, when he heard about Worsley's death, that there would be a fuss about it and people would probably think it was a murder ; and then whoever had been first home would get the blame."

" Oo," said Angela, " I like that. I see now what you meant the other day."

"We'd better cut that out. Yes, I admit the poor child meant well, but it was a clumsy thing to go and do, because it meant we both had to stand up in court looking perfect fools and telling quite inconsistent stories. However, I suppose it was just as well; because I got all worked up about it and forgave him; otherwise you wouldn't have had your nice race this morning."

It was soon time to break up the party; Angela was to come back to Lastbury, where no word was to be said to the Hallifords about the wedding, while Tollard waited for her at Hereford. From there they would race all the way to London; so insatiable were these ardent spirits of the unconventional.

Angela's first care was to unearth her husband and give him a breathless account of these new developments. It was disappointing to find him playing patience, because when so engaged he never gave any signs of strong emotion, or even of interest, and her excitement found no echo in his reception of the news. It was perhaps characteristic of him that the only part of her story which seemed to arrest him at all was one which seemed to her quite insignificant.

"So she hid in the dicky at the back of his car? Really, now, that's very interesting. That gives one furiously to think, does it not? I can't thank you sufficiently for bringing that

231

illuminating fact to my notice. Angela, if you will have the kindness to leave me alone till luncheon-time to finish my patience – I believe it is actually on the way to coming out – I fancy I shall have a rather interesting story to tell you this afternoon. I'm not certain, but I think so."

PHYLLIS MOREL LEFT as soon as they rose from
luncheon ; not without a promise to Angela
that they would meet soon. The Hallifords
drove off to a local fête, from which their guests
were mercifully excluded ; they scattered, as
they went, protestations of regret and an under-
taking that they would be back in time for tea.
The arrangement suited admirably, and they
were scarcely out of sight before the Bredons
were hurrying along the river path past the
boat-house, to join Leyland and to hold their
final council of war. Angela could get no word
out of her husband on the way ; " Leyland's
got to hear all this," he said, " I've made up my
mind on that, and I hate telling the same story
twice."

Leyland, it proved, had not been idle. When
Angela put him down at the drive gate, he had
professed to make for the inn ; actually, he
said, he had found a convenient hiding-place in
a copse just opposite the garage separated from
it only by a low hedge and a few yards of grass.
When the two women had gone in to luncheon,

233

he decided to risk discovery by stray farm hands and reconnoitre the garage for himself. The chief aim he had in view was to verify Phyllis Morel's statement that she had helped Tollard to empty his petrol tank : " you can't do that unless you've got the right kind of pump, and I wanted to see whether there was a pump like that on her car." It proved that there was, but, once in the garage, Leyland's detective instincts were too much for him, and he took a comprehensive look round, both in the garage itself and in an adjoining tool-shed. It was here he came across something which puzzled him and vaguely disquieted him ; a length of garden hose from which the nozzle at one end and the join at the other had been rudely hacked away, so as to leave a plain piece of tubing, perhaps twenty feet in length. " I didn't like the look of it," he explained ; " where I'd seen it before it always meant suicide with petrol gas. So I thought anyhow, if anybody was thinking of that, I'd spike his guns ; and I took the liberty of ramming a good round stone a foot or so down it, just in case of accidents. As you say, one doesn't want the suicide habit to get too common. But of course we might find that it has already served some purpose, if we could only discover exactly what happened on Tuesday night."

" I have," said Bredon.

" Ah ! . . . And I suppose you're going to keep it to yourself? Well, I won't complain, if that's your code. I've only made a fool of myself this time, and I don't deserve to get any pickings out of the business."

" I *am* going to tell you about it ; that's why I came here. Not because I think it's at all likely that it will enable a crime to be punished, but because I've a fairly strong idea that it may enable a crime to be averted. So it's the time for all good men to come to the aid of the party. Well, let me tell you first of all the whole business about the diary ; that's only just broken loose, so you haven't heard of it." And he proceeded to describe the loss and finding of the diary and the curious mutilations to which it had been subjected.

" There's been dirty work, that's clear," admitted Leyland. " But I don't see how we're to do much good without finding the missing page ; and I doubt if we're likely to do that."

" Oh, I'll tell you what was on the missing page ; not verbally but in outline. When Worsley had finished his description of the day's happenings, he added *I have put down my entry early to-night, because I am to* – and then he went on to say how he expected to end the evening."

" You mean he knew he was going to die ? " asked Angela.

" Not he. But he thought he was going to have a full and exciting evening, and that the events of it wouldn't be recorded till next day. It was in somebody's interest – you shall soon hear why – to destroy that document and conceal what his plans were for the next few hours after he wrote it."

" I suppose," suggested Leyland, " you mean that the document made it clear somebody wanted to murder him ? "

" No ; it would be more accurate to say it was destroyed because it made it clear that nobody wanted to murder him."

" Good Lord, man, you're not coming back to the idea that he met his death through an accident ? "

" Precisely. Through an accident."

" And no human hand brought him to his death ? "

" It's odd you should put it like that ; yes, strictly speaking no human hand brought him to his death. But look here, let's get this matter of the diary clear first ; because I warn you that it's of the first importance. I want to insist that there *has* been dirty work ; you can't explain it otherwise. That was a rotten idea, though of course I pretended to believe in it myself, that a housemaid would ever bother to put a book away in a shelf, when it had been left lying out on a writing-table. Hang it all,

Angela, I appeal to you, is that the sort of thing they would do ? ''

" No, you're quite right ; it's not their place. And of course they would know it wasn't a real book, because they'd look in it to see and find it wasn't printed.''

" Obviously. The book was removed, by some interested party, probably on the morning after the murder, for fear that it should be sent off with the rest of Worsley's things to his executors and possibly make trouble by revealing to them what Worsley's plans had been on the last night of his life. Now, why was it removed and then put back again ? Why not destroyed outright ? ''

Angela waved a hand and clicked the fingers of it in the manner of small boys who know the answer to a question in class. " Please, sir, I know sir. Because the book was in cipher, and until the cipher could be read there was no knowing whether it gave the show away or not.''

" Go up top. If the executors didn't miss the book, there was no harm done ; it could be destroyed later. If they did, its disappearance might look suspicious. Actually they did, and a letter came to say so, last Saturday.''

" You mean this morning.''

" No, I don't. The letter was read out to us this morning, but it came last Saturday. I'm afraid I have been nosing about a little, and I found that letter and noticed the postmark. On Saturday it became obvious that the book would have to be sent on. On Sunday morning, therefore, a rather ingenious plan was devised for discovering the clue to the cipher. A back page was torn out of the diary, was left lying about between the pages of a book, and became the subject of general discussion. That I would solve the puzzle was a fairly safe assumption. That was partly the reason, I fancy, why I was asked to stay on here. I did solve it, and I explained the principle of it to the Hallifords."

" Who then went and faked a new page ? "

" One of them did. And it was on an ingenious principle. Assume, for the sake of clearness, that the pages had been numbered – only the right-hand pages, of course, because only the right-hand pages were written on. Assume that the bottom of page 50 ended with the words, *because I am to*. Page 51 began with the words *take part in an eloping race*, or something to that effect, which it was necessary to eliminate. Page 52, naturally, was still blank. Pages 51 and 52 were torn out, page 51 was destroyed, and on page 52 were written the harmless words *to be blamed already for not obeying my doctor*, and so on. If only there hadn't been that little irregularity about the watermarks, it would have been difficult to discover the subterfuge, impossible to expose it."

" It might have been done more convincingly," suggested Leyland.

" It might, but time was short ; it had to be done on Sunday afternoon, and the ink had to be dry by Monday morning. Then came the question, How was the tearing out of the two pages to be made to look plausible ? Once more the solution was ingenious ; a blot was made on the back of page 52, and pressed down on to another sheet of paper, looking as if it had come by accident. Such a disfigurement evidently called for the removal of both pages. If only there had been no watermarks, the illusion would have been complete."

" Yes, there's nobody except the Hallifords in this," said Leyland, following the train of his own thought. " Which of them do you make it out to be ? Or both ? "

" Mrs. It was in her boudoir that I found the letter from the executors, with the postmark showing it was received on Saturday. And he isn't on in this, because don't you see, if he had been, the loose sheet of the diary which turned up yesterday would have turned up in some more probable place than between the pages of the book he happened to be reading. It's quite true that Worsley was interested in everything, and he might easily have picked up a book on fish-manures to glance at it, but he wouldn't have read it long enough, or with enough attention, to leave a page of his precious diary lying about in it. No, it was put in that book because Walter Halliford was reading that book and could not help coming across it and commenting on it. She wouldn't find it her-self ; she kept in the background – that was her way."

" But I still don't quite understand what she did it for," protested Angela. " If Worsley's death was an accident, why should she want to conceal the entry which showed how he meant to spend the evening ? "

" Because he meant to spend part of it in rather an odd place."

" Oh, don't be tiresome. Where ? "

" Well, in a space about three feet by three feet by five. As we ought to have known, really, when we found out what things he left behind in his bedroom when he went out, and what he took with him."

" You mean leaving his valuables behind ? "

" Not his valuables, but his breakable and droppable valuables. If a man curls himself up in a ball, to get into a small space, he will drop any coins or keys he has in his trouser pockets – but not anything he has in his coat pockets. And he may easily break a watch or an eyeglass, but he won't injure his false teeth. And there will be an undue strain on his braces, but not necessarily on his collar."

" I should have thought he'd have taken off his collar too, for luck."

" Yes, but he wasn't going to spend *all* the evening cooped up like that. And he wanted to look respectable when he came out. That's why he took a pocket comb, because you can't play sardines like that without ruffling your hair. Tennis-shoes take up less room, and scratch less, than shoes with nails in them."

" Very well, then ; she locked up Worsley in a coal cupboard or somewhere, I suppose that's what you mean ; and he died accidentally, same as the Mistletoe Bough. Do you really mean to tell us that she carted the corpse into a silo at dead of night and covered up all her traces, instead of explaining what had happened ? I shouldn't have thought it was possible for a person to go to all that trouble unless she was guilty of murder."

" Oh, but she is guilty of murder."

" I thought you said just now nobody wanted to murder Cecil Worsley."

" Nobody did. Least of all Mrs. Halliford. She murdered him by mistake for somebody else. That was the accident."

241

"THE ATMOSPHERE WAS all wrong from the start," he went on. "And the awful thing was, I knew it before the murder ever happened. But how could one have told ? Anyhow, Angela, you must do me the justice to admit that before we ever got to Lastbury I put the really important question – only you treated it as a rhetorical question."

"Such as ? "

"Why do these people want us to come and stay ? That was the point.[1] You see," he explained, "my wife, if she has a fault, is a tiny bit apt to be vain. And it didn't seem odd to her that these total strangers, who didn't in the least belong to our world, should be so desperately anxious for our company. She thought it was just for the sake of her *beaux yeux*. I, seeing the thing from a more dispassionate angle, felt at once we were there for a purpose. And when you are the official spy of an insurance company which has insured heavily the life – and for the matter of that, the house – of your

[1] p. 18.

host, you begin to see daylight. I was waiting
for something. Only what I was waiting for
wasn't in the least what came."

" It would have been very bad for you if it
had been," his wife pointed out. " You'd have
been quite unbearable."

" Anyhow, there was a coincidence, from the
start, which was too good to be true ; I felt it
couldn't be an accident that the Hallifords had
taken such a fancy to the society of a man
who happened to be the representative of the
Indescribable. And then, there was the company we were asked to meet. You yourself
realised, and told me so, that these people the
Hallifords had collected weren't really friends
of theirs. Therefore – so I argued to myself –
they have been asked here for a purpose ; Mrs.
Halliford is like that. But for the life of me I
couldn't see what the purpose was. If her plan
had come off, it would have been as plain as a
pikestaff ; but then it would have been too late."

" You mean," said Leyland, " that she wanted
to create an unfriendly atmosphere, so that it
shouldn't be surprising when things started
happening ? "

" Oh, no ; it was much more definite than
that. She was deliberately surrounding herself
with scape-goats. Her plan was so thought out
that it was almost certain the murder she was
going to commit would be regarded as the result

243

of suicide or of accident. But there was just the odd chance that the police might be suspicious and get on to the fact that it *was* a murder. If that happened, she wanted it to look quite clear that it was somebody else's murder, not hers."

" You mean Tollard ? "

" Tollard primarily ; he was scape-goat in chief. He had been mixed up in a murder trial in the States, and of course when that sort of thing happens too often it looks like carelessness.[1] So Tollard was given the post of danger, and the frame-up was against him. But look at the other people ; the Carberrys had known Walter Halliford in his less prosperous days in South Africa ; it was easy to imagine any old vendetta existing between them ; and Carberry, I suspect, has lived pretty hard. Then there were the Arnolds. They weren't the sort of people it's easy to plant out a crime on, but they were hard up, and they had expectations from Halliford.[2] It was just as reasonable to suspect them of having compassed his death as to suspect her. So there they were, you see ; a deliberate collection of possible suspects. That doesn't apply to Phyllis Morel ; she was only the bait used to bring Tollard there ; he was genuinely wondering whether to fall in love with her."

[1] p. 29.   [2] p. 32.

" It doesn't explain Cecil Worsley," suggested Angela.

" Cecil Worsley was there, I think, for a quite different purpose. He's a man whose character was beyond reproach, and he was a public man, with friends in high places. We are a democracy of course, and all that ; but there's a tendency, if you don't mind my saying so, Leyland, to hush up anything that is hush-able if important people are mixed up in a thing."

" Don't I know it ! " said Leyland, with a grimace.

" Very well then ; Worsley's presence would make the police more reluctant to turn the thing into a *cause célèbre*. It's amusing to think that in the event this very astute precaution utterly defeated itself. It was because Worsley was so well known that Lastbury became a household word in the British Press. She was a little too clever, was Mrs. Halliford, all through."

" Any more coincidences ? " asked Leyland.

" Why, yes, and the most obvious – the whole business of the eloping party. That copy of the *Babbler* hadn't been sent to the hospitals at all ; I found it afterwards in Mrs. Halliford's boudoir. There was nothing in it at all about concealing the identity of the elopers ; that was entirely her invention, and

245

she wasn't best pleased with Mrs. Arnold for nailing that particular lie to the counter. But it didn't matter ; the suggestion of secrecy, once made, naturally caught on, especially with the female of the species, who love thrills – all women love that rather silly game called Murder, because it gives them an opportunity of standing about and screaming in the dark."

" Here ! " expostulated Angela. " Miles, you really ought to remember your manners. And I didn't encourage the secrecy idea in the least ; it was only Mrs. Carberry and Phyllis Morel. Oh, by the way, Phyllis Morel did encourage the idea of picking one's own eloping partner for the reason I told you ; she wanted to carry Tollard off."

" How do you know, anyhow ? "

" Asked her."

" You always were shameless. She must be, too. Anyhow, complete secrecy wasn't essential to Mrs. Halliford's plan, though it would have helped. What was more important to her plan was all that fantastic business of making everybody go off to separate rooms ; and that wouldn't have happened if we hadn't been keeping the identity of the elopers dark."

" Was it worth it, though ? " suggested Leyland. " I mean, all that business of going off to different rooms – did she score much by it ? "

" Heaps. It meant that for nearly half an hour nobody had a strict alibi – anybody *might* have popped out of the house for five minutes or so unnoticed. Anybody, that is, except Mrs. Halliford herself, who took care to plant the representative of the Indescribable Insurance Company plumb beneath her window, and sang to him as she sat at it to make quite sure he realised she was there.[1] She also got her maid to come and sit there all the time,[2] so that if there was any idea of her victim having been murdered between half-past ten and eleven, there would be only one person with a perfect alibi – herself."

" And of course," Angela mused, " there was the whole atmosphere of conspiracy that evening, which made things easy for her."

" Exactly. When everybody is plotting in fun, you get a good opportunity of plotting in earnest. You can send people little notes, which they won't talk about ; you can suggest to them quite fantastic behaviour, and they look upon it as all part of the game. And then, of course, there was the race itself. King's Norton is an excellent alibi, when somebody is dying over at Lastbury. But it wasn't much of an alibi for the rest of the party, because in every case husband and wife were paired off ; there was nobody else to swear to their movements.

[1] p. 59.   [2] p. 150.

247

And therefore anybody who dropped out of the race by accident could be suspected of the murder."

" Like Tollard," suggested Leyland.

" Yes, but of course she took no risks ; she poured water into his tank herself – he was scape-goat in chief. Meanwhile, from the suicide point of view, what more likely evening, what more likely moment, for the self-destroyer to have chosen than the one evening on which he was left alone in the house with three hours and more at his disposal ? The idea actually crossed my mind at one time that Worsley did commit suicide, and that he had got Mrs. Halliford to invent the eloping party as an excuse for getting everybody out of the house."

" Yes," agreed Leyland, " the coincidences are striking, as you say, when one gets the clue to them."

" And, of course, there were added details which underlined them. For example, Angela, the first thing Mrs. Halliford did when she got you inside the house was to pour out a life-history of all our fellow-guests, bringing out just those points which made them possible scape-goats.[1] And then, all that business about the paper caps and the white favours at dinner was an eccentricity ; an eccentricity which, had we known it, meant danger. It was all part of the plan."

[1] pp. 29, 30, 32.

" Mmm," said Angela. " I don't see there was anything very extraordinary about all that."

" Not very extraordinary ; just a point or two out of the common. Other features of the plan *looked* absolutely natural. When your hostess picks up the post on the way back from a drive there is no reason to assume that she means to tamper with it, but she did.[1] And then, there were two subjects of conversation which meant nothing at the time but were enormously valuable when I came to work the thing out later."

" Let me think for a moment, and see if I can spot them. . . . No, no good ; I've no head for remembering conversations."

" You didn't hear one of them ; the other you can't have forgotten. When we were first shown out on to the verandah, Mrs. Halliford was being bothered by a wasp ; and, if you remember, she wouldn't kill it, or even let Phyllis Morel kill it, she hid it away under a cup. Her own explanation was that she didn't like seeing wasps killed because she couldn't bear scrunchiness.[2] Now, that was a very useful piece of self-analysis ; people tell the truth when their nerves are jangled, as hers were. She is the sort of person, you see, who had no real kindness about her ; indeed, she is fundamentally cruel ; but psychologically she's a

[1] p. 52.   [2] p. 26.

weakling, she recoils from the circumstances
of violent death, the messiness, the twitching
of the corpse. And that means that if she did
ever commit a murder, she would somehow
contrive to do it in kid gloves ; she would see
nothing of the agony, she would hear nothing
of the death rattle, there would be no blood,
no breaking of bones. Her part in the business
should be action at a distance ; there should
be a veil between her and her victim all the
time."

" Not a very easy kind of murder to contrive
without poison," suggested Leyland.

" Not at all ; and it has the further dis-
advantage, as the event proved, that it may
mean a fatal error in your calculations when it
is carried out. But she got her idea only a
short time ago, when she and her house-party
– another house-party – were playing after-
dinner charades. They did a scene from *The
Merry Wives of Windsor*, the one where Falstaff
has to hide in a clothes-basket and is carried
off and jolted, if I remember right, and left
lying in a muddy lane. Accidentally, I imagine
her husband was cast for the part of Falstaff,
and she saw her chance. Get a man shut up
in a box, when he thinks you're on his side and
you're really against him – what can't you do
to him, when once you've got him at your
mercy ? "

" Oo ! " said Angela, " now I'm beginning to get there."

" I know ; and when Phyllis Morel, at our end of the table that first night, recalled the performance of the *Merry Wives* and the incident of the basket, Mrs. Halliford didn't like it. She was afraid we might begin to get there before the thing had happened. So she turned to me quite suddenly and asked whether I fished.[1] No notice was taken of Phyllis Morel's remark at all."

" But you're not pretending you began to suspect, then ? "

" Good Lord, no ! But the whole thing, the whole chain of eccentricities in the management of the house-party, made me feel, as you felt, that there was something wrong. And we were right. All the preparations were being made, under our eyes, for the execution of a very elaborate murder."

[1] p. 37.

"THE POINT MRS. HALLIFORD discovered," Bredon continued, " is that the best mask for concealing a real plot is a sham plot. Perhaps it was the *Merry Wives* that suggested the idea to her. A man does not notice that you are plotting against him if you can make him believe that you are plotting *with* him. Once convince him of that, and he will obligingly tie himself up into a parcel, all ready to be despatched. And this tomfoolery people go in for nowadays, all this doorscraper-pinching business, is admirably fitted for the concocting of sham plots. That was Mrs. Halliford's opportunity. She was going to persuade her victim to tie himself up in a parcel, so that she could get rid of him without mess or noise or undue effort."

" You mean her husband, of course," said Leyland, who preferred concrete forms of statement.

" Yes ; it was her husband she wanted to get rid of. I dare say there's a good deal of history behind that which we shall never know."

252

" You think Cecil Worsley . . . " began Angela.

" Restrain your passion for sordid details. There's no need to speculate about the history of the woman's married life ; partly because she has already got rid of several' husbands without the necessity of killing them, partly because in this case the husband could only produce alimony if he were dead. Walter Halliford is nearly ruined ; if the world had been told that he had committed suicide there would have been no astonishment among those who really knew his circumstances. And it would have meant eighty thousand pounds in his widow's pocket. She couldn't wait for him to commit suicide ; she would help him out with it. Not a nice woman at all.

" She had got her house-party collected – the possible scape-goats, the witness whom nobody could suspect, and the representative of the insurance company which was to pay up. Into the middle of this party she threw the idea of an eloping race. And the sham plot was a plot by which she and her husband could win this eloping race hands down ; by a trick which could not very well be pronounced a cheat. If she had succeeded in getting her own private rule adopted – the rule by which the bet depended on the eloping partners successfully concealing their identity – things would have been easier.

As it was, she had to alter her plans slightly. She introduced a rule by which the eloping heroine must leave the front door with her escort not earlier than half-past ten, and the pursuers had no right to start until they had gone.[1] Those terms were carefully framed. The couple must leave the front door together, but there was no stipulation that both of them should be visible."

" Try and make it simple, Miles. You're puzzling Mr. Leyland, not to mention me."

" Well, let me put it for a moment as if the sham plot had been a real plot. Mrs. Halliford was going to drive off from the front door in public, at about one minute past the half hour, with her eloping partner *concealed in the car*. Thus, the rest of the company would not realise that the race was starting already. They would think that Mrs. Halliford was just driving up to the front gate, to look for her absent husband. They would be expecting her to come back and draw up her car in its proper place, ready for the race to begin. But in fact the race would already have begun ; once outside the gate, Mrs. Halliford would not come back. She would tread on the accelerator and make tracks for Hereford ; it might be a quarter of an hour or twenty minutes before the hounds realised what had happened and gave chase."

[1] p. 52.

"*I* should have called that cheating," objected Angela.

"So, for all I know, would Walter Halliford; but he knew his wife well enough to know that she was capable of that. In the first place, then, she had to arrange that she would draw the winning lot. There was not much difficulty about that. The lots, you remember, were on ordinary pieces of Lastbury notepaper; they were put into her bag – the sort of thing you call a purse nowadays, but it used to be called a vanity-bag – and shaken up there.[1] Well, this bag, like many others, had a flap in the middle which divided it into two compartments. Either compartment looked just alike. She put the lots into the right-hand compartment, let us say, and shut up the bag so that they could be shaken. When she reopened the bag, she was careful to reopen the left-hand, not the right-hand compartment; it's an easy trick, which nobody notices, and of course conjurers use it a lot. In the left-hand compartment were five folded pieces of Lastbury notepaper, which she had put there beforehand. They looked just like the real lots; the only difference was that they were all blank."

"Is all this guesswork?" asked Leyland. "Pretty smart if it is."

[1] p. 50.

255

" No ; she made a mistake. You remember, Angela, when she flourished that piece of paper in front of us with an E written on it ? She had put a full stop after the E. But the lot she really drew was, of course, blank ; she took it upstairs with her and drew an E on it ; if it had to be produced at an inquest, it would be well that her scrap of paper should have edges which fitted the others. She drew a fresh E, but she forgot to put in the full stop. I found that document when I took the liberty of going through some of her papers. It was just a silly bit of noticing work."

" Smart, though," added Leyland.

" Well, now she was in a position to go ahead. Having drawn the winning lot, her job was to communicate with her chosen cavalier, and tell him when and where to meet her. I am still speaking as if the sham plot had been a real plot. Accordingly, she had to send a message to her husband, which ran something like this : " Hide in the luggage-trunk[1] at the back of the Mossman at 10.25 to-night, snapping the lock after you. At 10.30 I shall drive off, and the others will not realise that we have started. When we are just out of earshot, I will let you out, and we will drive off to King's Norton together." The suggestion, utterly fantastic in itself, that a gentleman should shut

[1] pp. 51, 58.

256

himself up in a box at the back of a motor-car, becomes normal when you are in the mood for playing at adventure. And, in our overfed, disillusioned generation, that mood has become common."

Leyland was bursting with an obvious objection. "Why *send* a message ? Surely a message like that would best have been given by word of mouth. If people committed nothing to writing, what a hard time we poor devils of policemen would have ! "

"Well, from the point of view of the sham plot, there was no reason perhaps, but there was good excuse. You'll remember, Angela, the extraordinary atmosphere of secrecy that was going about the house that afternoon and evening. It was impossible to be seen talking to anybody in private without some officious fool looking over the hedge and exclaiming *That's them !* Actually, we kept so close together that it would have been difficult for them to get a word in private ; early in the afternoon, Mrs. Halliford was paying a call, and her husband was down at the silo. From the point of view of the real plot, there were three distinct reasons why it was best that a personal interview should be avoided. If you are going to commit a murder, it is not a good thing to have been seen talking mysteriously to your victim overnight. And again, a request sent in writing is much more difficult to refuse than a request made by word of mouth. If she had asked her husband by word of mouth, he would probably have said, " Nonsense, it's much too hot for that sort of thing." But we obey a command sent in writing to avoid the nuisance of having to answer. Meanwhile, there was a subtler reason, but one, I suspect, much more operative. The same squeamishness which made it difficult for Mrs. Halliford to murder her husband with her hands, or even to watch him die, made it difficult for her even to send him to his death by a spoken word. The written word is more impersonal, less part of us. Who does not prefer making a lame apology by letter, instead of blushing it out face to face ? No. Mrs. Halliford wouldn't see her husband die, and she couldn't have framed with her lips the words that sent him to his death."

" She was taking risks, all the same. What would have happened if Halliford had crushed the note into his pocket and it had been found on the body ? People are always doing that."

" Well, as a matter of fact we haven't found a line of Mrs. Halliford's writing which dates from that afternoon. I suppose she told him in the note that he was to destroy it ; after all, it looked like part of the eloping game ; if any of us had found it lying about it would have given the game away. And in any case, you see, if her husband had been found dead in the silo, she would have been the first person called in, and she would have been in an excellent position to go through his pockets before the police came. Anyhow, she must have written something of that kind. And, because she didn't want to have notes flying about, she conveyed the message rather ingeniously. She collected the post, when she was on the way home from her call, and smuggled away a circular, with the envelope unstuck, which had come for him that afternoon. It was an advertisement of some stuff described as Bechuanaland Tokay."[1]

" So *that's* why she called his attention to it at tea," exclaimed Angela.

" Yes, rather inartistically ; but she wanted to make quite sure that he read it. And now there was another job she had got to do. If her plan came off, she was to start in the eloping race, with a real partner, and so establish her alibi. Halliford, the imaginary eloping partner, would be dead ; she must choose another. She chose wisely ; Cecil Worsley would be the best possible kind of witness to have about you when you were establishing an alibi ; he was a man you would have left alone, without hesitation, in the strong room of the Bank of England.

[1] p. 53.

So she must write another note to Worsley, this time simply saying, " Meet me at the front door at eleven," or whatever the exact hour was. She adopted the same method of correspondence ; she looked out to find a circular which had come for Worsley, and the only one she found was the same Imperial fraud. I suppose everybody in *Who's Who* got an advertisement of Bechuanaland Tokay just then.[1] She wrote her second message on this, and put both circulars with the other letters in the hall. Then she went out on to the verandah ; she didn't call attention to the fact that she had collected the post, for fear it might arouse suspicion. Her maid, passing through the hall, opened Cecil Worsley's letter to see what it was about. I understand servants always do open letters ; the Lastbury servants, anyhow, are not particular."

" If they were mine, I'd fire the lot in ten minutes, bar the butler," agreed Angela.

" That was how the servants knew the house was going to be empty ; they thought Cecil Worsley would be one of the elopers. You'll remember, Leyland, how that puzzled us.[2] Of course, if the maid had opened Halliford's circular instead . . . But Mrs. Halliford didn't think of that ; for her, servants only existed when you rang the bell. She watched the

[1] p. 53.   [2] p. 123.

two men when they read their letters after tea,[1] some twenty minutes later and, seeing that both had read the contents of the yellow envelope, concluded that her affairs were well in train.

"But there were other preparations to be made. It was to appear next morning that her husband had met with an accident in the silo or had committed suicide. It did not much matter which ; the insurance money would have been paid up if the ordinary suicide verdict had been found. But on the whole it was better that it should look like an accident ; it meant less embarrassment generally. So traces must be left which suggested that her husband had just gone for a stroll before the race, that he had been tempted to walk into the silo, and there had been overcome unexpectedly by the fumes. She had stolen, before tea, his favourite and ordinary pipe ; an action which would have forfeited all my sympathy even if it had been her only base action that evening. It would not be difficult to create the impression that he had lost it that afternoon in the silo, and that he had met his death that evening in the search for it. It was a reasonable proposition ; a pipe is always worth looking for, and if he waited till next morning it might be lying under several loads of ensilage

[1] p. 53.

by breakfast-time. He usually carries an electric torch when he goes out at night; and he would naturally have it on him when he started for the eloping race; so a torch would be found, she assumed, in his pocket."

" But would the pipe have been left on the *top* of the silage? " objected Angela. " If he'd dropped it before tea-time, surely it would have got buried a bit? He pointed that out himself."[1]

" Yes, but we were probably meant to assume that he had fished about for his pipe and just succeeded in recovering it when he was knocked out by the CO_2. Anyhow, that's what she did; she went out after tea and dropped the pipe in the silo. Her way took her through the walled garden; and in the walled garden she planted out other clues, all meant to suggest that Halliford went out, late in the evening, in that direction. She overdid that part of the business hopelessly; the very number of the clues suggested to me that the thing was a frame-up. But, such as they were, they were ingenious. She dropped an old cigar-end close to the further gate of the garden – that was a good stroke. You see, anybody may be smoking one of his host's cigars *just* after dinner, but nobody is likely to be smoking his host's

[1] p. 53.

cigars at eleven o'clock at night. Inference – uncertain, but probable – that Halliford passed down that walk, calmly smoking a cigar, after the company had last seen him at about half-past ten."

"And the inference is surely strengthened," put in Leyland, "by the unlocking of the gates. Those gates are ordinarily kept locked – I had a prowl round that garden myself one night, and it meant climbing the wall."

"Yes, but it might have been an accident. To make things quite certain, Mrs. Halliford laid out crackers for dinner and, before doing so, took a cap from one of them and left it very obviously in the middle of the garden path. That made it certain that somebody had used the path *after dinner*. And the cap, actually, was of the pattern Halliford was wearing after dinner ; she arranged that by insisting on exchanging caps with him.[1] Of course, there's only a very limited variety of patterns, but it's the kind of evidence that *looks* very impressive ; *Why*, you say, *that's the very cap he was wearing!* And there was a final touch, still more ingenious, though less likely to be noticed. People who live in the country and take up farming as a hobby are for ever pottering round with rain-gauges and barometers and keeping records which nobody ever wants. Halliford, in the

[1] p. 81.

263

course of those evening walks of his, generally went to the maximum-and-minimum thermo-meter, took its readings for the day and set it for the night. So she did that, with the confidence that, if anybody looked to see, they would have no doubt her husband had set it in the usual way. She also put a pitch-fork just inside the silo, to look as if Halliford had been poking about with it.[1] Now, suppose every-thing had gone off all right from her point of view, and Halliford had been found dead in the silo with all those traces left about, wouldn't any jury, any coroner, have been forced to one conclusion? I mean, that Walter Halliford had left the party, fully intending to join in the eloping-race later on ; that, before doing that, he couldn't resist going out to the end of the walled garden, taking the readings of his beastly thermometer and setting it for next day ; that he dropped his paper cap by accident as he went down the walk, his cigar, nearly finished, when he was fooling with the thermometer ; that, having got so far, he thought he might as well have a look for that pipe of his in case he had dropped it in the silo ; that he took a pitchfork, swarmed up the hatches, found the pipe and was on the point of going home when, suddenly, he felt a choking at his throat and consciousness left him ?

[1] p. 172.

" Just possibly, suicide would be suspected. There was a still more remote possibility that murder would be suspected. To meet that danger, she poured water into Tollard's petrol tank, so that he would be exempt from the general alibi. Then she went back to the house and took her place at dinner. If she seemed nervous, if her hand trembled, who would worry ? The race had made all of us nervous that night."

" MILES," SAID ANGELA, " we all know you've got a loathsome habit of telling a story in your own way, which is usually back to front. But whatever Mr. Leyland feels about the thing, I just can't stand it. If you don't want me to scream, tell us now, in words of one syllable, how the two notes got mixed up. Because that's the mystery, really, isn't it ? "

" I wouldn't say it was the mystery ; I think we should have had a very pretty mystery if Mrs. Halliford's scheme had worked out according to plan ; the odds would have been about a thousand to one against our ever realising that anything was wrong – or, at least, against our finding out *what* was wrong. No, the exchange of notes isn't the mystery, it's the single touch of accident about the whole thing which tied it into a perfectly helpless knot. The scheme was so perfect that a single accident turned it all into a sort of bad dream. That's the worst of machinery, you see : it's most useful as long as it goes right, but once it goes wrong it goes so very wrong. Very few men have cut off their heads with their own swords, but plenty of people have blown their own heads off with fire-arms they were presenting at somebody else. Machinery, that's the trouble, can't correct itself when it starts going wrong."

" Monosyllabic, isn't he? Oh, Miles, for goodness sake get on with it."

" Well, Leyland, I told you just now that Worsley's death was due to an accident. You asked, did I really mean to say that no human hand had sent Worsley to his death? It was odd you should put it in that way ; I was able to say, quite truthfully, that no human hand had done it.[1] The operative word, you see, was *human*."

" Good Lord ! Not spooks . . ." began Leyland. But Angela had taken the point more quickly, and was wringing her hands in an agony of belated recognition. " Not that ! Oh, not that ! Miles, how perfectly odious of you ; I'm sure I could have got there all right if you'd led up to it somehow else. And the cut on the hand ! Oh, go on, tell him."

" The post lay there in the hall,[2] all spread out," said Bredon, " with the two yellow circulars, their flaps open, one addressed to Halliford and the other to Worsley. There was

[1] p. 246.   [2] p. 52.

a rattle of tea-things going on ; and this welcome sound attracted Alexis, the monkey, who associated it with eating bits of macaroon and sipping curious drinks which stung but were somehow vaguely pleasant. He prowled through the hall on his way to the verandah, hopped on to the shiny table and found all those white things lying about which made such good tearing. But no, there was a catch about that ; tearing them up meant being chased round the room and being shut up in a cage before it was dark, with people making angry faces at you.[1] He fell, instead, to imitating a trick he had seen human beings perform a thousand times – that subconscious trick of passing your forefinger round the flap of an envelope, scooping it open, and taking out the thing inside. Only one or two of the envelopes, the unstuck ones, yielded to such treatment ; but with these few it went well, and it was fun watching the thing inside flutter right down to the floor. He had done this three or four times, when he became conscious of a pricking in his finger ; he had caught it on the sharp edge of an envelope, and there was blood that wanted sucking off.[2] He was so engaged when Riddell, the butler, came through the hall and was confronted with the situation. He made a dash at Alexis, who was far too sharp for him and escaped chattering

[1] p. 27.　　[2] p. 54.

on to the verandah. Then he started putting the circulars back in their envelopes. Riddell, unfortunately, is a good servant, of the old-fashioned kind.[1] He does not read his employers' letters, even when they are open to view. The two yellow sheets plainly belonged to the two yellow envelopes ; they were plainly duplicates. If he had opened them out, he would have seen that there was manuscript writing on them ; he did not open them out. He put each back into a yellow envelope ; smoothed out the whole array of letters again, with the old servant's instincts of tidiness, and went about his duties. No harm had been done, so there was no occasion to report what had happened. He could hardly have been expected to mention it next day when he was interviewed by the police ; what earthly connection could it have with Cecil Worsley's death ? There was no concealment about the thing at all ; it was simply that nobody thought it worth mentioning until I questioned him, just before luncheon to-day, and then it all came out."

" I wonder it came out even then," said Leyland. " What did you ask him ? "

" Well, you see, I had got to the point of thinking that something of that *sort* must have happened. It all comes of playing patience, as I do when I'm thoroughly tied up. Somehow

[1] p. 44.

it draws a sort of curtain over the mind, and the jolly old subconscious gets loose ; at least, I suppose it's that. You stop running your head up against the brick wall, and approach the whole thing from a fresh standpoint which lets you see the gap in the hedge. Angela will tell you that's an illusion ; but anyhow it works. Up till then I'd been puzzling, as you were, over the impossible question : What have all these eccentricities, all these presumably fake clues, to do with the death of Cecil Worsley ? How do they lead up to it, or how were they meant to lead up to it ? But, when I started playing patience, the death of Cecil Worsley faded out of the foreground of my mind, and I saw all the other facts of the case in abstraction from it. And the moment that happened, you suddenly saw how all the odd facts hung together. They would only hang together if you assumed that they were leading up to the death of Walter Halliford.

" What I saw quite suddenly, quite con-clusively, was why the clues in the walled garden had been changed between the time when I went there before breakfast and the time when I walked there with Mrs. Halliford, about midday. When I was there before breakfast, and saw the opened gate, the regulated thermometer, the cigar-end, the paper cap, I felt instinctively that this was a frame-up.[1]

[1] p. 82.

They were not traces left by a man who walked in the garden overnight ; they were indications put there deliberately to make me think that a man had walked there overnight. But the person who had put them there was evidently dissatisfied with them, on second thoughts, and made a complete revision of them between breakfast and midday. And the revision was a curious one ; the cigar-end was removed altogether ; the thermometer was again tampered with, in such a way as to conceal the fact that it had been tampered with before. So far, it looked as if an effort had been made to obliterate the clues altogether. But, although the paper cap was no longer left at the side of the path, the white badge was left there instead. What sort of motive did such action betray ? It was the action, surely, of one who still wanted it to be thought that somebody had walked in the garden overnight, but wanted it, now, to look like a different somebody. The first idea had been to make it look as if there had been a visitor to the garden who was smoking a cigar, who was wearing a paper cap of a particular pattern, who was interested in maximum and minimum temperatures. The revised idea was to make it look as if there had been a different visitor to the garden ; a visitor who was at dinner – hence the badge – but was not wearing a paper cap, or not of that pattern ; who was

271

not smoking a cigar ;[1] who was not interested in the statistics which are the delight of the gentleman farmer.

" Who was the visitor suggested by the revised plan ? Surely Worsley, since it was his body that lay in the silo ; surely Worsley, since he alone, as a non-starter in the race, was at liberty to throw his white rosette away. Who, then, was the visitor contemplated by the first plan ? Quite obviously Halliford ; it might just be Arnold, but the chances were enormously in favour of Halliford. And that meant – what did that mean ? Somebody had, at first, wanted it to look as if Halliford visited the garden after dinner, and then had thought better of that plan and decided to make it look as if Worsley had visited the garden after dinner. The reason for the second plan was obvious – Worsley was the man found dead in the silo. The reason for the first plan, at that rate, was probably the same – *Halliford was the man who was meant to be found dead in the silo.*

" Once you saw that, you saw everything – the selection of the party, the suggestion of the eloping race, the clues left in the garden. The only thing which remained to be found out was, how the first plan miscarried. How did Victim A come to be substituted for Victim B ? Either because the murderer calculated, wrongly, on

[1] p. 71.

272

Victim B's known habits; or, much more probably, because the murderer had made some kind of assignation with Victim B, and the tryst had accidentally been kept by the wrong person, Victim A. A message going wrong – that was the obvious solution. Written messages are more apt to go wrong than verbal ones; how, then, could a written message meant for Halliford have reached Worsley by mistake? Messages delivered by hand do not easily go wrong; could it be, then, that this message had gone through the post? I decided to ask Riddell whether he had noticed anything unusual about the post that afternoon, and so blundered, by undeserved luck, on the story of Alexis and the envelopes.

"Anyhow, there was the situation at tea-time; there is Alexis, sucking the wound on his non-human hand; there is Mrs. Halliford, looking anxiously to see that the contents of both yellow envelopes are scrupulously read. There is Halliford, reading a message from his wife which tells him to be at the front door at eleven, to elope with her. He may have wondered at the choice, but not much; Mrs. Halliford was the kind of gambler who liked to win money, and, since it was pretty evident the Mossman was going to win, it would be a pity to divide the stakes. There is Worsley, reading a message which tells him to hide in the

273

big luggage-trunk just before half-past ten, and snap the lock behind him. It delights him to unbend his mind, taking it off the ramifications of European politics and concentrating it on the ramifications of a children's game. Children, that is what they were to him, these people of the Lastbury world ; adventurous, spoiled children. He throws himself into the situation, keeps alive, by constant sallies and innuendoes, the atmosphere of mock mystery. To-night, at half-past ten, he, the man who can travel to Geneva without a passport, will be playing hide and seek in the dark.

" So we get back to where we were before ; Mrs. Halliford goes out into the walled garden, plants her clues, and comes back to dinner. Everything seemed to be proceeding according to plan, and when Cecil Worsley got up and left the drawing-room[1] – abruptly, as his way was – she imagined that he really wanted to get on with his article, or that he wanted to rest before his midnight ride ; she had no idea, naturally, that he was preparing to keep the wrong tryst. What worried her was that her husband stayed on in the drawing-room, talking ensilage to Tollard and me, when he ought to have been making himself scarce in preparation for hiding in the luggage-trunk. If he left it too late, somebody might detain him at the

[1] p. 57.

last moment, and everything would go wrong. She concealed her impatience well – she had a mask of iron, that woman – but in the end she could bear it no longer, and gave Walter Halliford his clue by suggesting that he should go out and make sure the drive gate was open.[1] He did this, quite unsuspectingly ; then, as we know, he went down the river path to make sure that the gate there was shut and so calculated to delay the hounds a little. There was no hurry, from his point of view ; his next engagement was at eleven. He strolled along the river side, barely out of earshot from the front gate. Meanwhile, at 10.25 precisely, Worsley stowed himself away, uncomfortably but with the confidence that it would not be for long, in the luggage-trunk at the back of the Mossman.

" And indeed, in a moment or two Mrs. Halliford came out. There and then, with the whole party of us looking on, she drove off her victim, silent and helpless, through the drive gate and into the shadow of the silo. The next minute she was fumbling at the straps at the back of the car ; Worsley must have thought that this was the moment for his liberation. The luggage-trunk consisted, as they ordinarily do, of an inner and an outer case ; the trunk itself was substantial, made of good leather. The flaps

[1] p. 57.

both of the inner and of the outer case snapped to automatically when they were dropped into position, as Worsley had dropped them after him. That is the sort of thing that happens with a Mossman;[1] its makers appear to believe that their clients are bone idle cretins, who will never stir a single muscle unless it is absolutely necessary. But there were, of course, two separate locks, and you could open that of the outer case without opening that of the trunk proper. This Mrs. Halliford did, and hoisted the inner trunk on to the cradle, or whatever they call it, that hangs at one end of the pulley-rope. She shut the outer case, now empty, and made fast the other end of the pulley-rope, which had a hook on it, to the back axle of her car. All this time she was shouting " Walter ! " She must have been struck with a sense of dramatic irony, believing as she did that her husband was actually in the trunk at her feet. She would have been still more acutely conscious of it, if she had realised that her husband was in fact only a few hundred yards below, by the river, and that it was touch and go whether he would not hear the call and answer it.

" The rest was simple. She started up the car, and as it went forwards it took one end of the pulley-rope with it. The other end of the pulley-rope, with the cradle attached to it, was thereby hoisted into the air.[1] On and on she drove, until a faint slam behind her told her that the cradle with the trunk in it had reached the trap platform, pulled it up, risen above it, and allowed it to fall into place again. The luggage-trunk had been hoisted on to the platform in exactly the same way as the sacks of ensilage were;[2] the only difference was that Mrs. Halliford, whose strength would hardly have been up to a sustained pull with her arms,[3] solved that difficulty by using the engine-power of her motor. She called out her husband's name once or twice more, for the look of the thing, and then drove back to us, taking the end of the pulley-rope with her and dropping it close under the silo."

" But that's too awful," put in Angela. " Right under our eyes, when we were all laughing and playing the goat at the front door. I shall never forgive myself."

" Yes, it isn't everybody who can pull off a murder unnoticed in the presence, or at the least within earshot, of eight witnesses. Of course, he can't have died all at once. In fact, we know that he struggled ; tore his coat and loosed his collar-stud.[4] But, at that height, whatever muffled cries he gave must have been inaudible, though we were passing underneath in our cars all the time. I couldn't help

[1] pp. 23, 58.   [2] p. 24.   [3] pp. 25, 126.   [4] p. 70.

noticing, when the Halliford woman came back to the house, a kind of sinister self-satisfaction about the look of her ; I put it down afterwards to her confidence in the running powers of the Mossman. Well, she went up to her room ; kept close to her window so that I could see her as she smoked there ; sang a bit of a tune now and again to prove beyond doubt that it was she and no other who sat there with her maid, working. Then, at the appointed time, she made her way down to the hall, and came face to face with her husband. . . .

" She would have been a good client for the Indescribable. Can you imagine what it must have meant, the surprise, the disappointment, the mystification, the fear, all of which she had to conceal from her husband – from what she must at the first instant have thought was her husband's ghost ? With a superb reaction-time, she adapted herself to the new situation, hurried with Walter Halliford to the car, and drove it furiously through the night, thinking, guessing, planning like mad. She must have realised quite soon that the notes had gone astray ; realised who it was that was suffocating there on the platform at the top of the silo. She might save his life yet by a word ; but how could that word be spoken without sending her to the gallows ? Though she had time for thought, she had no time to think of a way of saving Worsley; every minute carried her further away from the scene where she was wanted."

" Yes, I see that," admitted Leyland. " But couldn't she have faked a breakdown, got away in the darkness, and opened the trunk before it was found by the rest of you ? "

" Just possibly. But then, for all she knew Worsley might be dead already. A breakdown meant that the race would be called off ; Worsley might be missed, the trunk might be seen. No, the best thing she could do to save her own skin was to carry out her original plan in this desperately altered situation. It meant losing perhaps the only creature she really cared for ; it meant that the best hope of rehabilitating her husband's finances was now gone, through her own act. But it meant, besides, that all her careful preparations had gone wrong. She had collected a party of scape-goats, and they were useless to her now ; nobody had any motive for killing Worsley. She had faked clues in the walled garden, difficult to remove in the darkness, and they were the wrong clues. And the remaining part of her plan was now much more difficult to carry out without risk of discovery. You see, if Worsley had been her passenger, she would have sent him straight to bed when they got back to the drive gate ; he was perfectly useless with a car. But Halliford would want to put the car away in the garage himself ; and that would leave the trunk high and dry ; how was she ever going to get it back again into position ? "

" How did she manage that, in the end ? "

" Fortunately there was the other car waiting in the drive, the Bridge. It was Halliford who put that away ; she must have sent him on ahead to do that, while she followed behind in the Mossman. Halliford, you remember, in his interview with the police told us something about that ; she got back to the house about ten minutes after he did, having had trouble in starting the Mossman.[1] During those ten minutes she was fully occupied. She had to swarm up the ladder, open the trunk, turn out, with averted eyes, its contents into the darkness of the silo, climb down, lower the trunk, fix it in position and garage the car. No doubt she did it all at top speed, for she could not be sure Halliford would not come back that way from the garage, instead of making a short cut, as he did, through the trees. There was just time to do that, and to remove the pitchfork, now a useless clue, from the silo.[2] There was no time to do the other thing that wanted doing badly – remove those fake clues in the walled garden. That would have meant a noticeable delay, so she left it over till next morning ; she trusted, mistakenly, that no intruding fool would pass

[1] p. 221.   [2] p. 173.

that way before breakfast. While we were still breakfasting she went into the walled garden, removed the traces which were now useless to her – the cigar and the faked thermometer reading, and substituted one of her white favours for the cap which looked like Halliford's. She had satisfied herself, somehow, that no white favour was found on Worsley's body.[1] Afterwards she walked me up and down the garden till I found her clue and pointed it out to her. Curse the woman, she made use of me right and left."

[1] p. 110.

" AND NOW WHAT ? " asked Angela.

" I'm wondering. I've put my case – Leyland, do you think it's a case for a jury ? "

Leyland drew hard at his pipe, with the air of a man who tries to find escape from an unpalatable truth. " Sorry, but I don't. Mark you, I'm just as much convinced by your story as if I'd seen the whole bally thing happen. But I don't see a jury sitting down under it. Fantastic, that's what they'd say. Lord, if you'd heard some of these defending counsel ! *I suppose you are an authority on fool's caps, Mr. Bredon ? Loud laughter in Court.* That's the kind of thing, and it makes you wish lawyers had never been invented. You and I can't prove that note to Worsley was ever written ; you and I can't produce that cigar-end. And what makes it worse, the one man who might be able to throw some light on the whole thing is the man we can't ask about it, Halliford himself. You don't think he's got any suspicions, do you ? "

" Not a hope. He'd be there in full force,

282

swearing his wife and he had never had a single divided thought ; and he the very man who was meant to be the victim ! No, you're right, it wouldn't do ; that's just the sort of dam' fool thing that would impress a jury."

" Well," said Angela, " that seems to bring us back where we were before. I repeat : and now what ? "

" I wish we knew," admitted her husband candidly. " The bother is, it's up to the other party to make the first move. And there's nothing so trying to the morale as hanging about waiting for events to break loose."

" I suppose it's certain something *is* going to happen ? We came away, Mr. Leyland, because one of the maids had to go off home. She's back now, and Miles seems incapable of allowing for my maternal instinct. Of course, if we're doing any good here——"

" Oh, that's all right," Bredon insisted. " I gather you really do admit now that the Halliford woman only asked us here because she had a dirty game on ? Very well then, if she asks us specially – me rather – to stop on longer, it means she's got another dirty game on. That's parity of reasoning. We know that she isn't worrying about her husband committing suicide ; on the contrary, if necessary she's prepared to do it for him. Therefore she was lying when she gave that as her reason for wanting me to stay ; therefore she wants me to stay for some private reason ; and why me ? Because I'm the Indescribable."

" Yes, but I'm dashed if I see that you're the indispensable. What's the good of having you about, except as a witness that the next little accident which happens is an accident and not a suicide ? And you told us yourself that even if it is suicide, the Company will probably pay up on a policy like this."

" Yes, but she doesn't know that. Besides, we don't pay up unless it's Unsound Mind ; and she's obviously beating up to that, with all her talk of nerves and the rest of it. No, she's Bruce's own spider, that woman, and she's just spitting on her hands for the next round ; you can see it in her eye, any moment."

" Oh, I expect you're right. But it does seem rather sudden ; I should have thought she'd have had the sense to rest a bit. What do you think, Mr. Leyland ? "

" I'm sorry, Mrs. Bredon, I'm afraid I'm on the other side this time. It is extraordinary, I admit ; but your real criminal who thinks he's deep never does wait long enough to avoid suspicion properly. Look at that boy in Scotland ; just escaped drowning in a scuttled boat one night and found shot next morning. Not that there was a conviction ; but it looked pretty clear from the police point of view. You see, for one thing Mrs. H. is all gingered up to kill, and she doesn't want to let her resolution ebb away. For another, the death of Worsley makes a plausible ground for a suicide in the family just now. And I think she's probably not quite absolutely certain that *he* doesn't suspect something. It's one effect of a guilty conscience that even when you feel you're on velvet so far as the rest of the world's concerned you're always afraid the victim may go and spot something. From her point of view, Halliford is just a mess that wants clearing up."

" M'yes ; there's something in that. But, as Miles says, it doesn't get us much further on if we don't know what her game is. She's not very likely to use the same waste paper basket this time, so to speak."

" Don't you be too sure of that, Mrs. Bredon. It's another extraordinary thing, how unoriginal murderers are ; how, once they've worked out a satisfactory formula, they think they can go on playing the same game *ad infinitum*. Look at the Brides in the Bath case, for example ; and that's one of a whole lot. I may be un-imaginative, as your husband always says I am, but I'm going to keep my eye on that silo for the next few days. She may have a new plan thought out ; but at least you have to be prepared for an actual repetition."

" I'm not so certain of that," put in Bredon.

" You see, she's a woman with an ingenious mind. I'd rather say that her next shot is due to be something *more or less like* the last, not something exactly like the last. Two accidents in the silo would be a bit thick, even for a jury. And, you see, there's one thing we haven't accounted for yet, when all's said and done – I mean that bit of sawn-off garden hose you found in the garage. That doesn't fit in with anything we've come across up to date."

" Oo, but I had an idea about that," said Angela. " You see, wouldn't Myrtle Halliford have wanted to prowl round a bit in the silo beforehand, just to reconnoitre ? And mightn't she, with the possibilities of spifflication constantly before her mind, have taken that bit of pipe along with her, leaving one end outside and blowing through the other ? "

" I don't give that suggestion very good marks. What sort of length would the piping be, Leyland ? "

" Too long for that, I'm afraid. Six yards of it at least. But I was going to say, mayn't the pipe have been part of some other scheme, which she'd thought out before, and then abandoned ? "

" That's possible enough. But then, isn't the idea she had thought out before and then abandoned almost certainly the scheme she will try to work off on us now ? Always supposing, of course, that it's feasible. No, I shall be surprised if that tube doesn't feature, somehow, in the next act. Lord, it's unnerving work, waiting for the next thing."

" Especially for you, my precious," Angela pointed out. " You see, if Myrtle Halliford is given to making these boss shots, it will almost certainly be you that are for it next time."

" I must apologise for my wife's macabre sense of humour. No, but seriously, we've got to keep our eyes skinned to a frazzle. You haven't come across anything queer yet, have you, Leyland ? "

" Pursuant to instructions received, we were always hanging about close to the bank whenever the man Halliford took a stroll by the river, which he's been doing pretty frequently. But, if you remember, you only told me to make sure he didn't commit suicide ; you didn't suggest I was to interfere in the event of his being murdered. Nor did you tell me to keep a look out for Mrs. H. ; and it seems to me she's the one that wants watching. The way you figure it out now, I'm not doing much good hanging about down here by the river."

" No, but I don't quite see where else you're going to camp. And if it's simply a matter of hanging about keeping your eyes open, I don't quite know that one place is better than another. Unless perhaps it's that road that goes past the silo to the farm ; I never can quite make out whether it's a public road or not, but everybody seems to use it. I say, we ought to be getting back, Angela ; tea's on. See you to-morrow, some time, Leyland."

The sky had grown overcast while they sat talking ; and by now there was a fine drizzle of rain that hushed the air and blurred the outlines of the trees, as if Nature were drawing a merciful veil over the horrors of Lastbury. To Angela, who had never had any love for it, the house now stood out as something definitely sinister ; she might have expressed her feelings, had she been otherwise brought up, by quotations from the Agamemnon. As it was, the phrase that kept passing through her head was " Won't you walk into my parlour, said the spider to the fly " ; she saw Mrs. Halliford, now, as a great blotched insect, always scheming, always taking advantage of you, behind her mask of banal up-to-dateness. Was she really sorry about Worsley ? Or was that, too, part of her rôle, the preface and the excuse to some fresh move in the game ?

It was Walter Halliford they found in the drawing-room when they went in for tea. He was consoling himself with Gilbert and Sullivan tunes on the gramophone, which he turned off, shamefacedly, when he saw his guests. Once more, he gave you the impression of being too

ordinary, too obvious-minded, for the grim
situation in which he was playing his unconscious part. He showed them an illustrated
paper with a picture of Worsley's funeral.
"I hate funerals," he said. "Seems so out
of place, don't you know, to make such a fuss
about planting out a fellow's body, which is
going to rot and all that. Worsley's been
cremated, of course ; much more sanitary, I
always think ; and yet it gives you the jimjams,
rather, the idea of being shoved through a hole
into an incinerator. However, I suppose it
doesn't matter much, once you're dead."

"Don't you think," suggested Angela, "that
anything up to date is always rather out of
place at a funeral ? I mean, whatever else
one's doing when one dies, quite certainly it
means joining the majority – *with the princes
and senators of the earth*, doesn't it say ? I'm
all for being behind the times on such occasions ;
I'd far sooner have the old nodding-plumes
business than be whisked away, like poor
Mr. Worsley, in a motor-hearse. Dying itself
is such a deliciously old-fashioned habit ; one
can't get over that very well."

"Well, I suppose I'm new-fangled enough
not to want to do it just yet, Mrs. Bredon.
Gosh, it makes you feel bad to think of being
bowled over all of a sudden, as poor Worsley
was. And it might just as easily have been me,

if you come to think of it. I suppose I'm sentimental, but I like to think of having a deathbed, and one's friends round and all that, and a last word or two to my old woman. Yet you never know ; it's Worsley to-day and perhaps me to-morrow. Hullo, Myrtle, here you are. Better have something to brace you up a bit. Mrs. Bredon and I haven't been having a very cheerful conversation ; all about murder and sudden death."

Mrs. Halliford's hand never shook as she helped herself to a cocktail. " That woman is all ready primed," thought Bredon to himself. " Things will be happening to-morrow."

NOTHING, HOWEVER, HAPPENED the next morning, except that Alexis the monkey went sick.

He lay, swathed in blankets, in a basket before a roaring fire in Mrs. Halliford's boudoir. The weather had turned again, and the heat was as bad as ever ; but Alexis, who seemed to have caught a chill from some mysterious draught during the night, lay there coughing hour after hour and shivering with fever. He was an even more embarrassing companion in sickness than in health ; his habitual air of depression left no opportunity for registering any change in his feelings, nor did he evince any gratitude for the attentions of his mistress. She was unwearying in these, flying to the door as soon as anyone came in, to shut it immediately, and putting up screens to keep off imaginary draughts from the window. " His poor chest's so delicate," she said ; " we *must* keep him wrapped up, or anything might happen. I couldn't bear to lose another friend," she added ; and Angela had the self-restraint to keep her hands off the sentimentalist.

By luncheon-time the invalid was no better, and Mrs. Halliford's insistence on a single topic of conversation had become wearisome beyond belief. The leading vet in Hereford, " the only man who really understands dear Alexis's constitution," was away on business, and it was doubtful when he would return ; would it be better to send the patient into Hereford to await treatment ? Halliford, discreetly supported by the guests, applauded this idea, but the prospect of being parted from her pet even for a day or two seemed to throw Mrs. Halliford into the vapours. In sheer pity for his host, Bredon invited him immediately afterwards to a long-promised return match at clock golf, and they were in the middle of a close contest when Mrs. Halliford bore down on them afresh.

" I can't bear it a moment longer. Walter, you will have to take Alexis in to Hereford. Walter, are you listening ? "

" What ? Oh, yes." There will never be complete understanding between the sexes until woman learns to make allowance for man's temporary absorption in the trivial. " Now, or when ? We're just in the middle of this ? "

" Oh, by all means finish your game while a miserable fellow-creature is dying by inches for want of help. I'd go myself, of course, only I've got the Freelands coming over. Look here, I'll go and get the car now ; and perhaps if you aren't too busy you could manage to ring up Jackson's before I come back, and tell them to expect you ? They are to have a fire lit, remember, and Jackson himself is to see Alexis the moment he comes back. And do hurry up with that absurd game, for goodness sake."

" All right, old girl ; I'll be ready any time. Here's the key. You know," he added to Bredon, " if my wife has a fault, and I'm sometimes doubtful whether she has, she's too dam' kind-hearted, that's what it is. This for the half, isn't it ? "

Bredon had begun to catch some of his hostess's impatience. He was particularly anxious to follow her up and find out what she was doing at the garage ; he was too much a man of his own theories to believe that the health of the monkey was, even now, the thought uppermost in her mind. Yet there seemed no reasonable excuse for abandoning the game while Halliford, postponing the urgent telephone call, went on with his interminable putting. Five minutes passed, ten minutes, and then, with something of a bad grace, the admiring husband bethought himself of his wife's instructions. " It's no good, Bredon, we'd better abandon the match. I must go and telephone now, or my name'll be mud ; and by the time I've finished she'll be back with the car. She must have been filling her up, to have taken so long. We'll play after tea, if that suits you." He sauntered in at the French window, and Bredon, as soon as he heard the telephone conversation open, made hurriedly for the garage. As he turned the corner of the drive, he saw a man coming towards the garage from the opposite direction, with a certain hesitancy about his air and gait. It was Leyland.

" Hullo, Bredon ; glad you've come. I've been hanging round, you see. Look here, there's something up. That big car's in there, with the door shut on it, and the engine's running. Anybody in there ? "

" Yes, Mrs. Halliford. Or it should be."

" But the door ! Why's the door shut, and the engine racing like that ? "

" The door's shut because she didn't want us to hear the engine running. Look here, you'd better keep out of sight for a moment ; I must go in and ask if I can help, or something. Unless it's locked, of course." The door – a blind, rather, of the roll-top desk pattern, covering the whole front of the garage – yielded to a touch ; and as he pulled it up a strong stench of petrol made him recoil in instinctive alarm. The great Mossman stood there, almost filling the narrow oblong chamber ; and in the driver's seat was Mrs. Halliford, her head leaning back against the cushions, her whole body crumpled up, with an unmistakable suggestion of death. What seemed to belie the impression was the brilliant complexion of her cheeks. Naturally she was pale, and what colour she had was unashamedly artificial, dashed on defiantly in hectic patches. Now, her whole face was suffused with a clear glow that put beauty into her features ; it was as if you were seeing her in health for the first time. Bredon looked round, and found the professional detective already at his elbow.

" Yes, that's what they're always like, these garage cases ; I've seen them before. Give it time to clear ; we can do no good, you know. Yes, that was what she wanted the piece of piping for ; it's in her hand, see ? I suppose she was going to shut herself up in the car and use that to let in the gas with ; then she found it was blocked, so she had to shut the door and stink out the whole garage. Here goes ! " And with a quick dash he made for the steering-wheel, started up the car, and piloted it out slowly into the open. The length of rubber tube dragged a little, then fell away from the car as it advanced.

" Can't feel the heart at all," Leyland announced presently. " The eyes still react, though ; there's just a chance, with artificial respiration. You'd better go and get *him* to

295

come down ; send for the doctor too, of course. You can't help here for the present."

" I was just wondering – oh, yes, I suppose one has to. I'll organise the servants a bit, too. I won't be ten minutes."

It was a relief to Bredon to find, as soon as he got back to the house, that there was no chance of finding his host yet. The vet, answering the telephone, had strongly advised that the monkey should not be moved ; he would come up to Lastbury himself if a car could be sent for him. The Bridge happened to be at the door, and Halliford had driven off in it at once, sending Riddell with a message to the garage to say that the Mossman could be dispensed with. Bredon sent him down with brandy instead, in case it should be needed ; for himself, he rang up the doctor, made a fruitless search for Angela in some of the main rooms and then returned to the garage. He stood with Riddell and one or two of the farm hands, watching in silence while Leyland still toiled on, true to his routine duty though without promise of success. " It's no use," he said at last. " No reaction at all now. Where's Halliford ? "

When the others had set out for the house in an extempore funeral *cortège*, the two friends remained, as if by common agreement, to discuss plans. Bredon took up the trailing piece of rubber tube, looked at it and smelt it. " Look here," he said, " we've got to get this clear. There's going to be another inquest, and you and I haven't left things as we found them. How did we find them ? And, more particularly, how did we find that piece of tube ? Was the back end fixed on to the exhaust ? "

" No, lying on the ground near it ; as if it had been tried on the exhaust and then thrown aside."

" Correct. And the other end ? "

" The other end was in her hand, or had been. The actual nose of it had been pushed back through that little hole in the glass, the one you shout to the driver through."

" So that if the gas *had* been travelling through the tube – we know it wasn't – it would have travelled right round the car, round the back of the driver's seat, through the hole in the glass, and so discharged itself into the back part of the car, not the front part ? "

" Yes, that's so. Seems a rum way of trying to do it."

" Depends what you're trying to do. And that's why you and I have got to have a conference. It strikes me that we have got to have a story to tell ; and we may just as well tell the same one."

Leyland frowned impatiently. " You're a queer chap, Bredon ; nothing ever seems to satisfy you. Surely to goodness here's a clean getaway, if ever there was one? I grant you, all sorts of things might have happened which would have made it necessary to tell all that story you told me yesterday, and probably be called fools for our pains. But now that the woman has been so obliging as to commit suicide under our noses, what's wrong with hushing the thing up and letting it go at that? There can't be any point in raking up the past now."

"Oh, we're going to say she committed suicide, are we? Good, that's the story I was proposing to tell myself. But let's get the whole thing taped. If she committed suicide, why did she do it and how?"

"Oh, as to why! Why does anybody? It's hardly ever the people you'd expect, apart from actual loonies. The one thing that does seem to make people do it is guilt; nearly half the suspected murderers do kill themselves, you know, which saves a heap of trouble. I suppose this poor creature's conscience worked a bit slower than other people's, that's all. And when you've not only committed murder, but killed the wrong person, and when your husband's losing all his money, I should have thought it would have been quite a suitable occasion, myself."

"Very well, pass the motive. *How* did she do it, then?"

" Well, she died of carbon monoxide poisoning, you can't get out of that. You don't get
that red flush from any other kind of death, do
you? And when a person who was all right a
quarter of an hour ago is found dead of carbon
monoxide poisoning, in a garage stinking with
petrol, in a car with the engine running, it's
normal to assume that a suicide has taken
place, isn't it? I suppose originally her idea
was to shut herself up in the driver's seat, and
introduce the fumes from the exhaust by means
of that piece of tube, which she's cut down for
the purpose. It's a favourite way of doing it, as
I dare say you know; makes it quicker, of
course, if you're shut up in a small space. And
those Mossman cars are very proud of being
absolutely draught-proof; so that if she shut
herself up in the driver's seat, with no hole
except just enough for the tube to pass through,
and the glass windows behind her shut tight
so as to cut her off from the back part of the
car, death would be a matter of a very few
minutes. But, as we know, the tube was useless
to her, owing to my happy thought in jamming
that stone into it. So she threw the tube aside,
and simply turned on the engine, keeping
the windows of the car open but the garage
door shut. It wouldn't happen quite so
soon, but in a small garage like this the time
of waiting wouldn't be excessive. That seems

299

to me a fairly reasonable account of what happened."

" Oh, reasonable, eminently reasonable. In fact, when you and I have faked the traces a bit, as we are going to do just now, it will be impossible for people to come to any other conclusion. But she didn't really commit suicide, you know – Mrs. Halliford. Let's fake the traces first, and I'll tell you the true story on the way up to the house."

" THESE WINDOWS, FOR example," Bredon went
on, " they don't look quite natural, somehow,
do they ? What I mean is, if you were sitting at
the steering-wheel of a car, in a closed garage,
trying to do yourself in with petrol fumes, you'd
let the windows on each side of you *right* down,
wouldn't you ? Naturally ; because that would
help you to a quick finish. We will just let
them down, so. And, though it's a small point,
you would want to keep the back part of the
car hermetically sealed, because you wouldn't
want to waste any of the fumes on that. So
you wouldn't leave that part open by so much
as a single chink – even the little round hole
through which one shouts directions to the
driver. We will shut that, don't you think ?
And now, this piece of hose-pipe. You've
accounted for its presence all right ; but, if we
are going to tell your story, I'm not sure that
it wouldn't be best out of the way altogether ;
it will only confuse the coroner. I think it
might be best if you put it back in that shed

where the lumber is kept, exactly where you last saw it. But first, I think we might get rid of that stone you shoved into it ; where is it ? Yes, it's some way down ; I think we'll just cut off a bit of the pipe, so, and get rid of the stone altogether. That gets the stone out all right, and we'll leave it on the drive ; concealing the weapon the crime was committed with, don't you know. And now, if you'll put the two sections of the pipe back where they came from . . ."

It was not a long walk back to the house, and as Leyland had no wish to appear in the proceedings as yet, he only accompanied his friend as far as the silo. The explanation, therefore, had to be a short one. " Let me add something first to your knowledge of the facts. That brute of a monkey has gone sick ; it may be an accident, but I rather suspect Mrs. Halliford left its cage in a draught all last night on purpose to give it a chill. They all have delicate chests, poor brutes. I think she was capable of trying to avenge Cecil Worsley. . . . Well, Halliford was to take it in to the vet.'s ; Mrs. Halliford was just bringing the Mossman round for the purpose. That gave an excellent excuse for having all the windows shut, even at this time of the year. As you say, the Mossman people are very proud of their tight-fitting windows.

"Now, I can't prove a word of what I'm going to say, but I'm pretty certain of it for all that. Mrs. Halliford went down to the garage in pursuit of a carefully thought out plan of her own. She fixed that length of hose on to the exhaust at the back and carried the other end of it round with her to the driver's seat. She opened the round hole which communicates with the inside of the car, and through that she put the end of the hose-pipe. She held it in her hand ; you could see she had been doing that when we found her. It was not the right size for the hole, of course, but by putting her hand well into the opening she could make certain that practically none of the gas escaped in her direction. Then she started the engine. She sat there, believing that the inside of the car behind her was filling up with the fumes. She noticed a slight smell, but that was natural ; it was not likely that the hose would be strictly airtight.

"In fact, she thought she was turning the whole of the back part of the car into a lethal chamber, full of deadly gas. When she'd done that, and shut the round opening behind her, she'd drive to the front door, instal her husband on the driver's seat and put the monkey in its basket beside him. Both windows, of course, would be carefully shut. But at the last moment she would warn her husband to fill up with petrol at the garage on the way out ; she had meant to, but forgotten it. He must keep Alexis shut away from all contact with the open air while he did so. She would wave her husband off ; and he, on reaching the garage, would open the window that communicates between the front and the back of the car, to put Alexis away out of the draught. That act would be his undoing ; the petrol fumes would rush through the opening and overpower him instantaneously. He would be left, probably, sitting in the driver's seat. There, a few minutes later, Mrs. Halliford would come to look for him, and would connect the hose-pipe with the exhaust again, fixing the other end of it somehow, through the floor-boards perhaps, to the front part of the car. Then she would go back to the house and announce that her husband had gassed himself in the garage.

" Of course, I can't be certain of the exact plot ; but that was evidently the kind of thing she meant to do. What she hadn't allowed for was the stone you obligingly jammed into the hose-pipe. The effect of that was that when she, sitting at the steering-wheel, turned on the engine, the hose-pipe blew straight off, and was no use for her purpose. The gas collected along the floor of the garage, till at last it rose high enough to overpower her unexpectedly where she sat. If she had only kept the garage door open !

But she shut it, for fear that the noise of the running engine would attract attention. There was no suicide. It was a second attempted murder ; the first plan was defeated by her own carelessness, the second by your carefulness – that was all."

" In fact, this time I'm the murderer ? "

" If you like to put it like that. I should have said the executioner. But you're responsible, anyhow, and you've got to make the best of it."

" Well, haven't I committed a crime, if you come to think of it ? If Mrs. Halliford's plot had come off, her husband would be dead and happy, let's hope, instead of being alive and quite certainly miserable. And she, instead of being dead with rather poor chances of happiness, would be alive and rich at the expense of your policy-holders. Neither you nor I would get any thanks ; but then, neither you nor I will get any thanks the way it is. Hasn't my interference been criminal, if it's meant so much less happiness all round ? "

" That's so like you policemen," said Bredon ; " the one thing you don't believe in is justice. Nothing could possibly be more just than what has happened this time ; the miscarriage of the plan brings death, not to a harmless stranger, but to the criminal. And it's your privilege to have turned the tap, so to speak, by which that

admirable piece of justice is administered.
Whereupon you immediately complain that
there is less happiness going all round, as if
happiness was what matters. You'd like all
the wicked to flourish, as long as they don't get
found out and give Scotland Yard the trouble
of arresting them."

" That's all very well, but if you come down
to hard facts my interference was a criminal
kind of interference. It was the kind of action
which did good, or so you say, but it might
quite easily have done harm, if Providence
hadn't taken over when it did."

" My dear Leyland, when you're my age –
that is, in about three years' time – you will
begin to realise that that is true of all human
actions. To go about scheming for human
happiness, as most people pretend to do, is
almost certainly to defeat your own end ; to
do what looks to you the right thing and damn
the consequences has the excellent effect of
leaving Providence free to take a hand in the
game. Of course you were right to jam that
stone down the tube the moment you suspected
that there was dirty work going to be done with
it, and – oh, well, don't let's argue. I must be
going up to the house."

They were standing close to the silo, where
the beginning of the drive parted from the
Hereford road. " Anyhow," said Leyland, still

lingering, " you're preparing to hush the thing up. Where's the sense of that, if it's all the triumph of justice you make it out to be ? "

" That's different," objected Bredon. " If you and I gave the whole show away, in the first place we shouldn't be believed ; so what's the use ? And in the second place, if we were believed we should only make poor Walter Halliford ten times more miserable than he otherwise would be. Much better he should mourn for a loyal wife than be kept awake at night by the thought of the narrow squeak he had, marrying a murderess."

" You believe in justice, then, but not in truth ? "

" Oh yes, I believe in eternal truth and all that. But mere truth of past fact, such as this is – why should anybody have a right to be told it ? Besides, it's all too improbable ; and I doubt whether the improbable ought to be told. It confuses people's ideas and makes them un-necessarily suspicious. In a case like this I'm ready to lie like – like a policeman."

And he ran down the path to the river, avoid-ing the house ; he would not be the bearer of ill news until he had seen Angela.

》》 If you've enjoyed this book and would like to discover more great vintage crime and thriller titles, as well as the most exciting crime and thriller authors writing today, visit: 》》

The Murder Room
Where Criminal Minds Meet

themurderroom.com

www.ingramcontent.com/pod-product-compliance
Ingram Content Group UK Ltd.
Pitfield, Milton Keynes, MK11 3LW, UK
UKHW040434280225
455666UK00003B/54

9 781471 900457